Deception of One

Introducing Detective Charles Wilson

Donovan Smith

ISBN: 979-8-37-603236-7

Dedication

This book is dedicated to my wife, Taylor, and my son, Declan, for all their love and support.

To the readers: I hope you have as much fun reading this book as I have had while developing and writing it over the past ten years.

Finally, this book is intended to inspire all of my former Soldiers, friends, and family members, and, of course, the Breathe University and Lions Not Sheep family members all around the world that anything is possible if you buckle down, stay focused, and work hard to achieve your goals and dreams.

Acknowledgments

First, I would like to thank my beautiful wife, Taylor, for always being there for me and keeping me focused on the task, from reading multiple rough drafts of the book and providing feedback on the book cover to entertaining our son to ensure that I could finish this passion project of mine.

To my son, Declan, thank you for always being the light in my life and motivating me to strive for greatness. We have been through a lot together in your young life, but it will be worth it in the end.

I would also like to thank the late and beautiful Sue Grafton, author of the "Alphabet Series" featuring Detective Kinsey Millhone and her family. When I started writing this book in 2009, I had no idea of which direction to take the book after multiple rewrites. After being blessed with the ability to have a phone call with the great Mrs. Grafton and having her review one of my final manuscripts, I knew exactly what to do with this novel and where to take Detective Charles Wilson.

Lastly, I would like to thank all my friends, family, and Soldiers who continuously pushed me to finish this book and constantly asked me when it was coming out. Well, after 10 years in the making, the book is finally complete, and I thank you all for choosing it.

About the Author

Donovan Smith is a United States Army Intelligence Warrant Officer and a family man. He resides in Colorado with his wife, Taylor, their son, Declan, and their three dogs. He was born and raised in the small vineyard town of Lodi, California. He graduated from American Military University with a Bachelor of Arts in Intelligence Operations/Homeland Security. Looking to further his knowledge, Donovan enrolled as a graduate student at The Pennsylvania State University, where he is pursuing a Master of Professional Studies in Homeland Security.

Donovan has a long history of community service. He volunteered with the Special Olympics and the Pearl Harbor Memorial Foundation as an undergraduate. He is also actively involved in his local community as the head coach of two Fountain soccer championship teams: The Bombers and The Cobras. When he is not writing, he can be seen coaching his son's little league teams and going on travel adventures with his family. He also enjoys outdoor activities such as camping, hiking, and running with his dogs.

Donovan began writing his debut novel after winning multiple California Student Poetry contests in high school and discovering his passion for crime and mystery novels. He loves writing and wants to share his work with the world. If you're interested in more of Donovan's work and learning more about his life, check out his website at: *https://donovan.webversatility.com/*

Contents

Dedication i
Acknowledgments.. ii
About the Author iii
Chapter One – A House Call in the Sticks....................1
Chapter Two – One for the Books 19
Chapter Three – Coroner's Office 41
Chapter Four – The Suspects 51
Chapter Five – The Suspects' Residences 59
Chapter Six – The Arickson Residence 83
Chapter Seven – An Unexpected Turn 98
Chapter Eight – Endless Possibilities 123
Chapter Nine – A Rude Awakening 132
Chapter Ten – The Evolution of a Monster 148
Chapter Eleven – The Truth Shall Set Them Free.....165
Chapter Twelve – Can You Make One......................188

1

A House Call in the Sticks

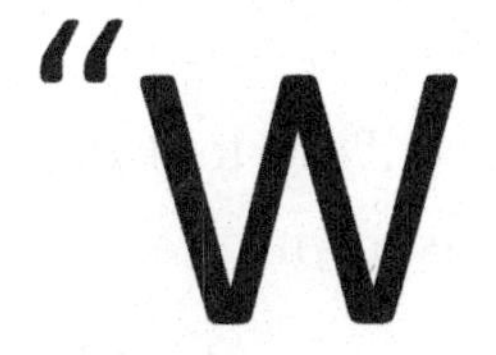ilson, come in. Over," the voice crackled over the radio.

Detective Charles Wilson glanced down at the radio in his car. He was exhausted. It was getting late, and he just wanted to head home for a hot shower and a glass of scotch. Exhaustion carved lines onto his handsome face. The days at the office seemed to get longer and longer. He was suddenly reminded of the time he eagerly received his first badge. He didn't love his job any less now, but somehow it was like an old marriage—a familiar partner that you needed a little break from. His mouth let out a long, weary sigh, thinking that he could ignore the radio and that the call might go to someone else. It wasn't possible. He just wasn't wired that way, but he could not find the strength to reply.

"Wilson!" The voice repeated, "Do you copy? Over."

He frowned, staring at the radio. He was not going to keep Laura waiting. He'd known her for years; she was like a sister to him. Like any sister, she wasn't going to get off his back until he did what she said.

"Wilson here; what's up, Laura? Over."

"What's your twenty? Over."

Wilson rubbed his eyes; he didn't like where this was going. The workday was supposed to have ended by now, but he knew Laura well enough to know he was in for a long night.

"Down off Rural Route Seven. Over," he told her. Whatever it was, he prayed it was across town.

"Perfect," she said, and Wilson's heart sunk. "We have a call out that way. I need you to take a look. Over."

"Call? I'm not up. Richard is. Let him take it. Over."

"Not an emergency call," Laura said. "Disturbance call. Out at the abandoned place by the twelve-mile marker. You know the one, I mean? Over."

"I know it," he said.

It's fate, Wilson figured. *The moment I want to take a break, I get called to a creepy-looking house in the middle of nowhere.* Wilson already knew what he'd find: either the homeless or misbehaving teenagers.

"I'm not sure why you're calling me, though. Get a uniform up there. That's what they do. I've got the gold shield now. Remember, I don't have to hoof through underbrush chasing a startled deer? Over."

Laura sounded exasperated when she came back on. Wilson knew he was going to end up paying for being hard. Still, there was a principle at stake.

"Shift change," she said. "No one can be up there for thirty or forty minutes at best. Over."

"It's a false alarm," he told her, trying to keep his voice steady.

The call was likely not an emergency, which is why he was trying to escape it. The last thing he needed right now was to get snippy with Laura and make her angry. She had a way of remembering these things and maximizing his guilt. She also had a sneaky way of making him pay for it. Plus, it wasn't her fault that he was exhausted.

"Somebody got spooked by nature, and now that person's making it our problem. Over," Wilson added to sound a little more agreeable.

He was certain that was what it was. It seemed foolish to squander his time and energy when he was already running low.

As he'd predicted, Laura scoffed and told him off. Wilson often wondered if Laura got some sort of joy from his pain. Well, maybe not enjoyment, but more like a sadistic pleasure. He wouldn't put it past her. At this point, she was more of a cop than most cops he knew, right down to the morbid sense of humor.

"Chief says to do it, so do it. Over," Laura said, in a tone that assured Wilson she wasn't going to budge.

He had no choice. Stubbornly arguing might be a fun way to piss off Laura, but he knew the consequences would far outweigh the fun. Wilson groaned, pulled a U-turn, and headed back the way he came.

It wasn't just exhaustion; he deliberately didn't want to go, which was weird. He couldn't remember ever being unwilling to do his job. He knew the seriousness and importance of the job, but something felt off, and it certainly wasn't the exhaustion.

Despite his feelings, he gunned his car's engine and headed toward the scene of the disturbance. Perhaps, the reminder of his responsibility made him go.

"Ten-four, dispatch," he muttered into the radio. "Leave the lights on; I'll be looking for coffee and an apology when I get back. Over."

"Copy that," Laura replied, the smile back in her voice. "I'll have the coffee ready. Over and out."

He grinned and signed off. Of course, Laura didn't say anything about apologies. Doing so would mean admitting she was wrong, which she didn't know how to do. In all the time he'd known Laura, he'd never seen her apologize. She took the blame with an ironic smile and found a way to correct the mistake, which was one of the reasons he held her in such high regard. Wilson had learned the hard way that taking responsibility was significantly more effective than apologizing.

The road leading to the crime scene was empty and dark. A dozen or so houses were sprinkled here and there in the area; none of them were night owls. They all looked sad. It didn't seem like the kind of place where you'd want to raise kids. Each house he passed was a little darker than the last. He could've been driving around at the end of civilization, and it wouldn't have been much different. Wilson wondered if he'd find the edge of the world if he drove a little further. His brain, ever the artist, conjured up the image of him driving off the edge, plunging into nothing. For a moment, his imagination was so vivid that he felt weightless.

"What's next, Charlie? Gonna join a cult and prepare for an alien invasion?" He laughed, trying to keep his spirits up.

The road still stretched ahead of him. On either side of him lay endless fields dotted with trees everywhere, not a single sign of humanity anywhere. The houses, though he knew they were occupied, appeared abandoned. He glanced at the sidewalks, noticing a spider web of cracks that made him wonder when they were constructed. Wilson looked out and saw a blurred figure in the distance. He squinted, realizing a second later that the blur was nothing but a scarecrow.

Needed just that, Wilson thought, peaking at the scarecrow.

The more he thought about it, the more he realized his instincts were right. This area was the perfect spot for teenagers and drunks, and nine times out of ten, it was some scared homeowner who saw a shadow passing through their fields. However, there were other possibilities too. The reason this place attracted teenagers made it the perfect place for someone to hide a body. He shook off the morbid thought; exhaustion usually turned him into a pessimist. With each passing day, Wilson felt himself losing faith in humanity. To be honest, it could be said that this job had made him cynical and pessimistic; the dark neighborhood didn't help with the case either. The mental images of the most heinous crime scenes he'd worked on lurked in his mind.

He was now deep in his thoughts, remembering the effect of this place on him. Why would anyone even want to live here?

Hmm, so nobody can hear their victim's screams? His mind reacted readily.

His guffaw broke the silence. "Of course, that's why."

However, now that Wilson thought about it, the whole situation did feel off. The houses in this area were so far away that they didn't even come into view. By the looks of it, there were no more houses left. So, who called this in? Who was out this far to notice something at the abandoned house? What were they doing so close to the house in the first place?

As far as he knew, it wasn't a popular place among lovers for a full-moon nighttime stroll. They could be hoping to sneak in a little quiet time, but why would they choose the creepiest-looking house around? Campers were another possibility, but the season was all wrong for that. It was cold enough to freeze your balls off; only a lunatic would risk it.

Again, Wilson rid himself of the morbid thoughts and hoped to find either a bunch of stupid kids having a party or an old drunk, so he could shoo them off and get back to his plans for the night.

He was sure he could handle the teenagers, but the drunks were less predictable. Sullivan, his training officer, ended up with two broken fingers and a bruised testicle after going up against a drunk. All of this occurred in broad daylight in the middle of Main Street! It was five o'clock in the afternoon, and there was a large crowd of onlookers. Who knew what some guy would do way out here at this time of night? Especially one who was crazy and desperate enough to break into a house that had everything apart from a sign on the front door that said, "This place is haunted… in case you haven't already figured it out."

Wilson was in no mood to find out how a testicle gets bruised, which inwardly made him shiver.

"Are you at the scene yet, Wilson? Over."

The radio crackled with the voice of Laura, the dispatcher, breaking the silence in Wilson's town car. Her voice broke the monotony of his thoughts.

"Less than a mile out, I think. This place is in the sticks, I'm telling you. Over."

"Yeah, I checked the map. It looks rural," Laura said. "Watch out for coyotes and hillbillies out there. I hear you don't want to run upon either of them in the dark," she said half-jokingly. "Over."

"Be careful now. You know, my mom's side is full of hillbillies," Wilson said in a mock-serious tone. "There's nothing wrong with being country folks. If living in the city has taught me one thing, it's that it doesn't make someone more civilized than a guy out here. Over."

Now that he thought about it, he would be glad to find hillbillies out here compared to a murderer — or a drunk.

Laura chuckled. "Isn't that the truth? Over and out."

Wilson scanned the area around him as he drove down the two-lane road…he noticed it was deserted. As he peered ahead, he noticed his reflection in the rear-view mirror, making him frown.

Damn, I look older, he thought, examining the wrinkles at the corner of his eyes. Some might think they were smile lines, but they were a product of his constant squinting. His eyes glazed over the other lines etched on his forehead, but he fancied that they added character. He knew people who joined the force alongside him and now looked dead in the eyes. They saw too much pain and suffering, which didn't let them move on.

"At least I've got a full head of good hair," he said, a ghostly smile playing on his lips.

Wilson was coming up on forty, but it was hard to tell if the lighting wasn't just right. He was tall with steel-blue eyes, featuring his long-cut face and salt-and-pepper hair divided into unequal sections, making some strands fall and mess around his short forehead. He could be said to rarely get insecure about his appearance, often earning him a good reputation among the ladies. The fact that he painstakingly made sure that he remained lean and fit didn't hurt either.

Wilson's thoughts came back to reality as he reached the abandoned house. His body language changed almost immediately. He was alert before, but he knew that he wasn't in any real danger. Now, he was focused.

"You about there, Charlie? Over."

"Pulling in now, dispatch. You know, I hate it when you call me Charlie. Over."

"Okay, Charlie. Keep me posted when you get inside. Over."

"Will do. Over."

Wilson's headlights bounced off the gravel driveway, reflecting off the tall Johnson grass. The grass swayed slightly in the breeze, which would help mask the movement if there was any real threat. He felt the sense of foreboding get worse.

He drove ahead, his lights finally falling on the old, abandoned house at the end of the drive. At first glance, the house looked exactly like it was supposed to; all but two windows were smashed in. The wood siding was so dark that it blended in perfectly with the night, and there was a gaping hole in the roof, which Wilson could see from his car. The perimeter of the building was littered with shards of broken glass; the remnants of alcohol bottles thrown in frustration at the end of the bottle.

Wilson parked the car and stepped out into the chilly night air, his senses on high alert and his hand ready to reach for his gun at a moment's notice. He studied the shards of glass closely and saw a relatively unbroken piece that resembled a crack pipe. It wasn't unusual to find a crack pipe in the middle of nowhere, but he pitied the guy coming here to smoke crack.

Wilson walked toward the steps leading up to the porch. The door itself hung lifelessly, like a torn limb attached by just a ligament, and the frame was falling apart. The night sky and the house looked like they came straight out of a horror movie, sending chills down his spine. This unusual place was making him uneasy. He took out his flashlight and announced.

"Police! Is anyone there?" he shouted at the top of his lungs.

No answer.

"Alright then, I guess I'm allowed to go in," Wilson whispered, unsure whether it was a good or bad thing.

His wish of finding kids partying here seemed to be going down the drain. Years of experience in the force had taught him the importance of gut feelings, and his gut was uneasy.

He stepped over the threshold, and the sound of crickets chirping welcomed him inside. Apart from that, there was utter silence. The house didn't look habitable at all; the insects made sure of that. The interior was simple enough: the main door leading to the living room, an open kitchen, a bedroom at the opposite end, a staircase leading upstairs, and a pathway leading to the other side of the house. Nothing looked too disturbed, which could be taken as a good sign.

Wilson stepped into the house, which made the floorboards creak. The foundation of the house had grown weak over the years. He flashed his light on the ceiling, and the entire structure looked like it was holding itself together through willpower. The chances of anyone hiding upstairs without making a sound were slim. Wilson searched the house only to find broken furniture, rats, and what looked like human feces.

He stepped out, facing the yard, after making sure the house was empty. The yard looked abandoned, but he knew he could only be sure by checking the soft ground for footsteps.

Walking the perimeter of the property in search of anything out of the ordinary, he found nothing apart from a brown wing-tipped shoe near the porch, which was old enough to lose all significance. Inside the broken-down, four-foot-long chain-linked fence that ran the perimeter of the house were mounds of garbage; plastic bags from gas stations, brown paper sacks used to hold pints of cheap liquor, random pieces of paper, disposable cups, drug paraphernalia, and used syringes caked with blood. The most bizarre thing Wilson found was surgical tubing, which he decided to bag for evidence.

Weeds had woven themselves through the chain-link gate like an earth-and-metal quilt, rusting the chain link in some areas. The debris on the ground made it evident that squatters used the house infrequently. Not recently, but at some point. A couple of them might even be here, hiding in the tall grass or the fields beyond the house. Or they'd all run away when they saw a car drive up to the house. The latter was the likelier of the two possibilities. However, he couldn't just leave the site based on an assumption. He needed to find the person who had placed the call.

Wilson returned to the front of the house and stood in front of his car. He had left the lights on but rolled up the windows, took out the keys, and pocketed them. Then, he walked through the gate at the end of the driveway, leaving it ajar so that if anyone tried to open it, the sound would alert him. He pointed his flashlight at the house, taking a moment to thank God he didn't live in a place like this.

He walked into the field, checking the ground around the house to see if any footsteps were leading away, but with no luck again, he frowned, concluding that the call might've been a prank.

"Is anyone there?" he called out. "I'm not here to arrest anyone. I just need to know what's going on out here. If you are in there, come out with your hands up where I can see them."

Wilson waited a minute or two and listened for any rustling inside the house. As non-confrontational as his shout had been, he doubted anyone would jump out to show themselves since the place appeared empty.

The silence grew maddening, making him notice that even the insects had gone silent as if sensing something ominous. He shrugged, deciding to give Laura a piece of his mind for wasting his precious night and delaying his plan. However, the fact that he hadn't found the caller bothered him. He scanned the area again, carefully trying to see any unusual disturbances. Nothing seemed out of place. That was that.

"Guess that's that. All clear."

He shone his light on the field one last time and headed back to his car. He made it to the overgrown path leading out of the drive. Just as he was about to sit in his car, he heard a strange sound, like some metal crashing to the ground. He drew his 9mm Glock pistol, trying to locate the source of the sound.

Now, Wilson was sure that he wasn't alone. How had the person managed to stay so still? Wilson's gut told him that the sound originated in the back of the house, so he started for the backyard. The person there already had the advantage of knowing where he was, whereas Wilson was looking for him.

He knew the darkness shrouding the night would help conceal him if he was smart. So, he slowed his footsteps, his eyes scanning all possible threat points. Adrenalin flooded his veins as he anticipated dangers from all around.

He made his way to the backside of the house, where he noticed that the grass around the house was flat. He had been in that spot a moment ago, which meant that the person had come toward the house from outside. Now, there were three possibilities. Either the person saw that he was about to leave and made a loud noise to try to stop him, or they made a mistake, or the floorboards just breathed in their last breath. Logic hinted to Wilson that the second option made the most sense since the third just seemed like wishful thinking, and if the person was trying to find him, why would they still be hiding?

He scanned the surroundings, his eyes straining to see any sign of human life. There was nothing. His gaze lingered on the house for a moment before he continued moving.

Wilson diverted his attention toward the house. He walked up the porch, his hand reaching for the door to push it open, when he realized his flashlight was still out.

He clicked it back on, abandoning his attempts to remain hidden. For a second, he toyed with the idea of calling for backup before abandoning it. He remembered Laura telling him about the upcoming shift change.

"This is the police," Wilson called out again. "Come out with your hands up, or I *will* shoot."

It didn't surprise him that nobody came out, as it would have been surprising if they had.

He stopped and tried to listen but heard nothing other than the random sounds the crickets made here and there. Slowly entering the kitchen, he noticed the backdoor at the opposite end. He walked over to it and turned the knob, caked with dirt and grime. There was no creaking on this door.

This was most likely the door the person used to move about, which meant they knew it wouldn't make any noise. That meant they frequented this place often. He labored to keep his breathing slow to calm his racing pulse. Out of the corner of his eye, he saw a shadow move. Instantly, he whipped around in that direction, only to find a half-torn curtain swaying in the breeze.

Get a grip, Wilson!

He then headed for the bedroom, his eyes constantly on the lookout for threats until a flicker of light caught them. It came from the passageway leading to the door Wilson realized he'd missed. He presumed it went down to the basement.

Taking a deep breath and holding it in his lungs, he crept toward the light. A disgusting smell filled his nostrils as he moved closer to the light. It reminded him of raw meat gone bad. Wilson wondered if there was a corpse somewhere in this house. The smell teased his senses, lingering. It made his stomach roll with sickness. As the smell grew stronger, Wilson was sure there was a faint hint of dried blood.

He had always been against violence, which was one of the reasons he joined the police force. However, he had to face plenty of it in his line of work — but that was the price he paid to live his life according to his morals. Eventually, violence became familiar, and he found some comfort in that, too.

Etching closer to the light, Wilson's grip on his pistol increased and loosened. The flicker of light was finally clear, and it appeared to be a flame coming from a large candle placed in the center of the family room. The gutted floors and the striped walls still had traces of a floral pattern. He let his breath out slowly as he walked toward the candle.

It's probably just some bum or runaway, wondering if he was consoling himself. After all, he shouldn't be surprised if he eventually found out that this was a ritual carried out by a cult. In general, people were crazy. The smell was the blood of animals.

Wilson reached the hallway that led to the other side of the house. It was an enormous area, falling upon itself due to the elements. The smell of rotten wood mingled with that strange, pungent, metallic aroma somehow made the smell worse, which Wilson didn't think was possible. The wood on the walls and floor was rotted to the core, with termites crawling out. As the flashlight shone across the place, smaller holes were revealed in the wood where insects had eaten away the flooring.

The eerie smell seemed to get stronger. He knew it. It teased his senses with the familiar stench of blood. He still didn't have a full view of the room, but from what he could see, there was no one near the burning candle. There wasn't a shadow anywhere; the place was dead silent. Wilson then walked closer to the partially rotted doorway. As he swung around the corner, the barrel of his gun following his eyes, he felt his blood freeze in his veins. He was right in thinking that it was the smell of blood, but wrong when he thought it was the blood of an animal.

2

One for the Books

Wilson finally blinked and could feel his blood starting to move in his veins again. As life came back to him and his limbs thawed from their frozen state, he collapsed, still clutching his gun.

"Oh, my God," he whispered, his eyes facing his hands. "Oh my God, what the hell is this."

His words were coming out in the form of loud wheezes. He pressed his palms against his face, trying to blot the image out. It felt like it was engraved into his eyelids. Even when he closed his eyes, he could still see it. Wilson's voice rose in anger and disgust; he felt sick to the core. If he'd looked in the mirror, he would have seen his skin turn to a sickly shade of green, his eyes wide with horror and shock. They had a glazed overlook that screamed terror at what he had just witnessed. His stomach rolled in dizzying swoops, which felt like vertigo but worse.

Finally, he got the chance to pull himself up from the floor and get himself together enough to try to make it back out to his car to call for backup. Bile rose in his throat again, threatening to spill over. His urge to throw up was getting wilder. As he stood, his eyes again fell back on the gruesome scene he had just walked into. Nearly collapsing again, he grabbed the wall for support, but the wall gave way and sent him crashing to the floor. Tiny insects ran across his skin. Usually, insects didn't bother him, but these made him want to claw out of his skin. The world spun around him. His tongue stuck to the roof of his mouth, trying to get out the smell of blood that crawled down his nostrils into his throat. He shook his head as his sight faded in and out, making him think that he might faint any minute now.

"Get it together, Charles," he told himself firmly. "Just get to the car. You've got to get to the car."

With that, he took the first shaky step, followed by another, trying to steady his breathing. But it seemed like it wasn't quite working, as the breaths he took were getting stuck in his throat.

"Just a few more steps. You'll be fine. Breathe."

It was slow at first, but his breathing seemed to even out. His entire body was still shivering, but he felt like he was in control for the first time in the past twenty minutes.

Detective Wilson had been on the task force for fourteen years, and by now, he had seen countless suicides, homicides, and freak accidents that had left people with severed limbs or bashed-in skulls. However, he had never, in his career, seen anything come close to what was in that old, abandoned farmhouse. As he stumbled through the shadows of the house, he shook his head from side to side, trying to shake loose the images that had burned into his brain. He jogged through the overgrown yard, and his feet felt like they were magnets, and the ground was a refrigerator door. His legs were trembling. Even in his delirium, he wondered how they supported his entire body. He wanted to crash to the floor in agony. His head felt full of sand, and his tongue seemed to swell in his mouth. It was every nightmare he had ever had, rolled into one. He fought for control throughout the walk and was slowly winning the battle, putting all his years of fieldwork to use. He strove to be as stoic as he could be. This one touched him; it completely threw him.

Finally, he got to the car and held on to the edge of the door like it was a lifeline. That link to normalcy steadied his heart and his breathing. He snapped out of his daze as the cold metal gave him a comforting sensation. Grabbing the speaker in his hand, he spoke in a rushed tone.

"Laura? Over," panting into the radio, he crumpled into a pile in his driver's seat, dropping his head into his hands. He didn't want Laura to hear just how distraught he was. *Pull yourself together. Don't let them see you sweat.*

"You find a cousin out there in the boonies? Over," she asked in a light and joking tone. She was completely unaware of the horrors he'd witnessed.

That natural sound of her voice helped a long way toward regaining his lost rhythm. For close to thirty minutes now, he'd felt off-center. He slowly began righting, knowing he'd never be the same, not ever again.

"Laura, I need backup at once! Over," he wheezed out the words.

At least he didn't sound scared shitless again. The thread of urgency was firm this time; she must have picked it up.

"Charles, is everything okay?" she asked, her tone completely changing now. "What's going on? What is it? Over."

"Send backup immediately, Laura. This is — it's the worst thing I've ever seen. I don't know how someone could even think of doing something this horrendous. Just… I need backup immediately. Please. Over."

She'd picked up on how destabilized he was. He'd forgotten that there was no hiding something that big from her.

"I'm sending backup, but I need to know what it is, Charlie." Laura waited for a response, and when there wasn't one, she added, "How many people do you need, and what's for them to know? Over."

"I am at Thirteen Fifty-Two Green Valley Road, on the outskirts of Wine Valley. I am going to need a few officers out here and for the Chief to be notified. And send out the coroner's van, too. It's a homicide, a gruesome homicide — an entire family. Over."

He managed to keep his voice steady throughout the report, biting the inside of his cheek hard enough to draw some blood. He was trying to catch his breath. The metallic taste had him resisting nausea that suddenly washed over him. Wilson chuckled darkly under his breath. He'd thought he'd been exhausted before. He now knew what exhaustion meant; it felt like years had been shaved off his life. He put his head on the steering wheel and took a deep breath.

"Holy…" Laura said, just above a whisper.

She had witnessed a lot of unfortunate events over the years as a dispatcher, so it never ceased to disturb her when she heard something like that. But right now, goosebumps broke out all over her skin. Charles sounded so broken that all she could do was try not to break down on his behalf. It was more than a shock to see him this affected and horrified over the radio. Detective Wilson was one of those hard nuts the department has always been proud of. He was smooth, impeccably dressed, and rock-solid; nothing fazed him.

"And tell them to prepare themselves beforehand because this will not be easy to stomach. Over."

In that decayed house, bathed in their blood and the dim yellow light of one solitary candle, were five lifeless bodies covered with deep, intensified cuts and gashes. The separation of skin from flesh left strips of meat hanging down the sides of their bodies. It looked as though some crazed psychopath had come in, wielding two machetes, and just started spinning circles around the family. Each body was precisely sliced with such brutal savagery that whoever had done this had been having the time of their lives.

In Detective Wilson's experience, murders like that were the basis for the sensational blockbusters Hollywood produced. They happened in real life, but not often enough to make a regular cop like him think he'd ever seen such a thing. It would never have even crossed his mind. They were sure to pray against cases like this because they were the ones that could break even the most hardened of cops.

The images of the bodies were enough to break him. Their faces, arms, legs, and abdomens were slashed so many times that there was more blood and muscle visible than skin. The intestines spilled out of the abdomen like pale, wet ropes that were slimy with blood, digestive food, and whatever the hell it was that should have stayed on the inside. The bone stood stark in contrast with all that blood—pale ivory with a glistening wet core. Wilson couldn't block out the bright white of the bone. The five mutilated bodies dangled from the rotting ceiling of the house by a nylon rope.

The only foundation bars still standing were the ones that held them to the roof. When he got close enough, Wilson realized that the bodies belonged to the world-renowned Arickson family. Their faces were contorted in silent screams of agony. The frozen look of pain on their faces confirmed their death was dreadful. He couldn't even begin to imagine the pain they might have suffered or the fear they would have felt. He could get the idea of what their last moments on earth would have been like, with no motive that could explain this.

The Arickson family was more than just a family; they were a household name. They were iconic. The patriarch of the family, Steven Arickson, was a billionaire who made his fortune inventing an anti-virus computer software called Fireburner, which was light-years ahead of its competitors. The software would scan computers within seconds, whether they were home computers or government computers, and destroy the most complicated and discrete viruses hiding on computers. This allowed users to enjoy advanced security on their computers. Steven Arickson had found a way to sell people time, and time sold better than non-alcoholic beer at an AA convention. Five years after the software hit the market, almost every computer had it installed. Within a decade, it was famous worldwide. Mr. Arickson had made enough money to care for his great-grandkids seven times over.

Steven Arickson had spent a good part of his life as a spindly, waifish fellow, a little on the pale side and not too concerned with fashion or being hip. He was an inventor, a thinker, a brain server — nothing close to a rock star or an athlete. As a child, Steven conducted science experiments in his garage while the other boys played baseball. When he became a teen and his peers started dating, he began building robots for fun in his spare time. To put it short, he was never popular with the ladies. However, after the Fireburner became such a success, Steven Arickson's love life changed quite drastically, as you would expect.

Steven began dating and soon married a supermodel, Lisa Anne Potter. She was about an inch taller than her husband and a bit tanner. While Steven was always pasty white, sun-kissed, Lisa Anne was always glowing.

Watching them together, many often scoffed and grumbled to a spouse or whoever stood nearby, "We don't have to wonder what she sees in him, huh?"

As unlikely a couple as they were, and although his money probably did play some role in their union, Lisa Anne was madly in love with her nerdy half. He was different from the movie stars and the professional athletes she had dated, and she found great comfort in the disparity. She also loved how his mind worked and all the little quirks that made him who he was. It was a real-life Beauty and the Beast situation, but it worked for her. She thought she had found her happily ever after.

The Aricksons had their first child, Trey, less than a year after their nuptials. Four years later, they had a daughter named Katy, and five years after that, they had their last child, Sky. The blissful parents wondered how their children would turn out with such diverse genes. Before becoming a model, Lisa Anne had been an All-American volleyball player; her father was a professional football player, and her grandfather was an

Olympian. When they found out they were pregnant for the first time, the two imagined together what their firstborn would be like.

"He may have brains *and* brawn," Steven said as they awaited Trey's arrival.

Lisa Anne said jokingly, "Like the Hulk."

"Or something a little less volatile, I hope," Steven quipped.

Every moment of the Aricksons' lives was fodder for the media. Every cheap supermarket tabloid had someone on the payroll who could feed them tips and quotes. Sleazy websites had a dedicated Arickson page, complete with an e-mail address for tipsters. They were not only rich and fabulous, but they were also incredibly private. This made the media hungrier for any information that they could get their hands on. There was not a single piece of the Aricksons' lives that wasn't picked over and scrutinized by anyone and everyone. Even the smallest, most private conversation could end up being the subject of an article. The mundane shopping trips. Front-page news. There were ridiculous headlines and wild speculations about the real nature of their relationship. Then there was the recurring gold digger rumor; it always amused Lisa.

As it turned out, their first son did indeed inherit his mother's athletic genes. In his senior year of high school, he led his team to a state championship and was subsequently offered full-ride scholarships to several Division I universities. The kid hadn't even reached college yet, but he was already known for his talent. Charles had seen him play countless football games, as he was an avid high school football fan.

***

Charles stood outside the house and took a few drags of his cigarette while waiting for backup to arrive. He kept his pistol close at hand, and his ears pricked like a skittish mule on a mountain hike. He was optimistic that the killer was gone, but he knew better than to get too comfortable when dealing with a maniac who could hack an entire family up like a street-side butcher—to the way the bodies had been displayed. The killer had been trying to send a message. For the life of him, Charles couldn't figure out what that was supposed to be. His brain felt like it had been put through a blender.

Before putting out the cigarette on his car and stuffing the butt in his pocket, Wilson took one last, deep drag off it. Having done that, he reached inside the vehicle to get his camera and some evidence bags. As much as he didn't want to go back in and face the once-beautiful family that now hung lifeless like slabs of beef in that dim family room, he knew that he had to go back into the house—into the gore—so he could start gathering evidence while he waited. A case like this would be time-consuming, and he knew that every minute counted if he wanted to catch the murderer, which meant he needed to get to it.

He slowly walked back into the room and surveyed his surroundings again. The scene was just as shocking as the first time. The smell hit him again. He gagged but held it together. The team was going to get there soon. He couldn't be losing his cool when they did. It was his case now; he had to get his head back in the game to crack this one wide open. There wasn't much optimism following the observation. Only a determination not to screw up.

"I remember watching him play football," he said to himself as he glanced up at Trey and shook his head.

The boy had been so full of life and energy. His youthful vigor had to have leached out of the figure that hung. His body looked like an unbelievably detailed wax effigy. Something that had never known life and would never know it again. Trey didn't look like a human. Not anymore. Wilson knew it was hard to separate the victim from the human he had been. It would have been easier to handle, but Wilson didn't distance himself from the harsh truths. Here was a boy who lived. Who had his life snuffed out of him?

"What a tragedy. What happened to you? To all of you?" he whispered with an almost reverent tone.

As Wilson started taking photos of the crime scene, he noticed something he hadn't seen before in the dimness of the room. Just behind the victims' lifeless bodies that hung like morbid piñatas from the rafters of the house, there was writing on the wall — large, sloppy letters that spelled out, ***"Only one sinned, but all had to die."***

The words were gummy and almost black. At first sight, it looked as though someone had smeared raspberry preserves onto the wall with a butter knife. Detective Wilson knew that there was no jelly used to pen this disturbing note; it was written with the five victims' very own blood. It was solidified and caked on the wall in a maroon parody of graffiti.

Wilson pulled a handkerchief from his pants pocket and took several deep breaths as he squeezed his eyes shut so tightly that every muscle in his face ached. Catching his breath, he opened his eyes again, returned the handkerchief to its pocket, and continued to take photos. As Wilson bent down to snap a shot of the entire scene, a subtle noise broke the silence in the house and set alarms off in his head. He heard the faint scratch of the back door on the old linoleum floor. Wilson dropped the camera and yanked his gun from its holster. His skin went cold, and his breathing became shallow. He quickly pressed himself against the nearest wall and waited for the next sound. There were footsteps. It sounded like multiples. There might have been more than one killer, and they might have been back. Wilson held his breath and waited. The footsteps grew closer and closer until….

"Wilson? Are you in here?" a voice echoed throughout the old house.

Wilson recognized the voice of Detective Richard, a reasonably seasoned colleague who specialized in homicide. He holstered his gun and let out a breath.

"Toward the front of the house," he called back.

"Holy shit," a rookie officer named Jason Cooper said as he turned the corner into the room. "This is…"

"It's the worst you'll probably ever see, newbie," Wilson said, finishing the sentence.

"You got any ideas about who might have done this?" Cooper asked as his eyes shot to the floor in an attempt to avoid the victims' death-stricken faces.

"If I had any idea, I'd be the best detective you've ever met, Cooper," Wilson grumbled. "I've been in here for a few minutes taking photos. What the hell might I get out of three minutes? This isn't like in the movies, Coop. It takes more time than that."

Damn, those crime shows. They gave people the idea that horrible cases like this were wrapped up within an hour, with space in between for commercial breaks. Wilson knew he was short-fused, but it was hard to be patient in this situation.

"Sorry, boss," Cooper apologized. "I've just never seen anything like this."

"Neither have I, kid," Wilson replied, softening his tone. "As I said, this is one for the books. Stuff like this doesn't often happen."

"Thank God," Richard said as he sifted through some trash on the floor near the hanging bodies. "Wilson," Richard said as he knelt to pick up something from the floor. "Here's something."

"What?" Wilson inquired, still snapping photos.

"It looks like a broken picture frame."

"What's the big deal about it? There's broken stuff all over this house."

"This one has a picture of the whole family; only the mister and missus are ripped out of it."

"Put that in a scene bag, and we'll have it fingerprinted and analyzed back at the lab."

It was too early for speculation, and focusing on one thing could limit the investigation, but he couldn't help his train of thought. Was jealousy a reasonable motive?

"That's why I like having you on the job, Richard," he said as he snapped a picture of the writing on the wall.

"You got gloves, Coop?" Richard asked his new partner.

"Yes, sir."

"Put 'em on and start collecting, then."

Cooper pulled out a pair of white latex gloves from an evidence kit and slipped them on, fumbling with the fingers as he did. He slid the broken frame into a bag they used for crime scenes and labeled the piece of evidence. He handled the frame like an overfilled martini glass as if too quick a movement might destroy the thing. Something about Detective Wilson made him uncomfortable. There was no way he was going to do something stupid again.

"I'm going to go ahead and put the broken glass in a bag as well, just in case there are prints on the pieces," Cooper announced, keeping his eyes trained on the glass he was slipping into a second-thick plastic bag.

He looked up and couldn't help staring in open-mouthed horror. He couldn't believe that this stuff happened in real life. "Who in the world could have done this?" Cooper muttered as he glanced up from his task at hand to the victims. The question came out before he could stop it. He slipped a glance at Wilson to see if he'd annoyed him again.

"I have no idea, but they knew what they were doing," Wilson quietly responded, focusing on the ominous message left behind.

He wasn't annoyed. He'd been thinking the same thing. What level of craziness would anybody have to wreak this kind of havoc on a human being, and that too on children? He didn't think the person behind this could even be considered human, as this was some next-level monster shit.

"I can't imagine someone so twisted," Cooper said, shaking his head.

"You'd better get used to dealing with twisted people if you plan on sticking to homicide," Richard said, warning the newbie.

"I'll tell you one thing," Wilson chimed in. "I will bring any person with a mind to commit something so evil to justice as long as I have a heartbeat."

"Maybe the guy just had some serious anger issues," Cooper replied with a bit of a chuckle, trying to make his mentors laugh.

"That's a family of five there, Cooper. Three of them have probably never even had their first love yet. You need to work on timing if you want to be a comedian, kid."

Cooper's eyes shot to the floor as he mumbled an apology and got back to work.

"How do you know a guy did this?" Richard asked.

Cooper was glad for the change of subject.

"Well, I'm just gauging by the tightness of the ropes and the cuts and slashes on the bodies, and I'm considering each person's weight. I know that Arickson is a skinny dude, but that's a good hundred and seventy pounds, and the kid is probably pushing two hundred. I'd just think it would have been impossible for a woman to lift them and hang them from the roof like that unless she was some kind of bodybuilder," Cooper replied, with some self-satisfaction for having been so clever.

"However, two questions remain," Wilson remarked. "Who did this, and how was the perpetrator able to get the entire Arickson family here to hang them up like slabs of meat?"

At that moment, two people from the coroner's office — a short, stocky man and a woman who looked like she ran track in college — entered the house. The three men called them back to the scene.

"Get the bodies down and put them in separate body bags," Wilson ordered.

Cooper and Richard cut the bodies down from the roof as the two from the county coroner's office waited to bag them.

"Man, they're heavy," Cooper grunted, struggling to take Mr. Arickson down. "They're already pretty stiff."

Once they had cut the five bodies from their nooses, the officers, with the help of the other two, carried the bodies out of the room one by one and placed them each on the front porch, where they slowly placed each of the mutilated corpses into separate body bags. Even with five people on the job, it took half an hour to get the Aricksons' bodies packed into the body bags. The bodies were loaded into the coroner's van and hauled to the coroner's office so that each one could undergo an autopsy to find the real cause of their deaths and, hopefully, something that might give Wilson and Richard any leads.

"You got even an inkling of an idea?" Richard asked as they wrapped things up at the scene.

"Not even a smidgen. But I will, and I will put the psychotic son of a bitch where he belongs."

"Interesting," a voice was heard from behind Wilson. "That'd make some quote."

He didn't even have to turn around to know who it was. Already, he felt his stomach acid bubbling and his fists aching to clench. And, for the first time, it occurred to Wilson just how bad this could all get.

He turned slowly. Standing a short distance away, almost tucked into the shadows, was a short, slight woman, around thirty-five or so — though she could easily be mistaken for a little kid if you didn't look closely enough. She was dressed for hiking, with a heavy peacoat that almost swallowed her up, flashing him her famous *I know everything you don't want me to* grin.

"Marquez," Wilson stated flatly.

Richard, that sly bastard, had already slipped away. Gloria Marquez slid a reporter's notebook out of one of her pockets and flipped it open with practiced ease. A pen appeared in her hand as if by magic. And she did have some kind of magic, didn't she? Wilson had seen seasoned cops, guys who wouldn't flinch at anything, freeze up under that wide-eyed, all-seeing gaze of hers.

"Evening, Detective. A bit late, huh? Shouldn't you be home by now?"

Wilson shrugged, "Maybe I'm just sucking up some of that outrageous overtime pay. I seem to remember somebody writing a whole series on how it was like an epidemic in the department."

He saw her flinch just a little, which made him feel good. She had screwed herself when she wrote that series. As a reporter, you could get away with a lot. Cops knew better than to bother taking it personally. But you screw with a man's overtime, you cross a line. She'd been feeling the effects of that stunt for a while now. Unfortunately, she was enough of a pro not to let it get her too rattled.

"Lotta guys out here, I notice."

"Think so?" It was all Wilson would give her.

She arched her brow, "Am I wrong? Is that how you're playing it?"

"I'm not playing anything. Games are not really my thing."

"No?" she inquired, smiling. "What a shame. Games are sometimes fun, you know?"

He wasn't going to take the bait, "What're you doing here, Marquez?"

"You know what I'm doing here," she said, all business now. "Care to comment?"

"You know, that's not going to happen."

She scribbled something in her notebook before looking back up at him silently. He knew the game. You go silent. The first one to talk is the loser — yet another trick he'd seen work on many guys who should have known better. He tilted his head and crossed his arms, letting her know he wasn't going to be the one to break.

To her credit, it was several minutes before she finally gave in with a sigh.

"You know it's going to come out. You're better off getting in front of it."

"That right?" Wilson said. "Well, I appreciate the offer, but no thanks."

She shook her head and slid the notebook away, "Have it your way." With that, she started walking toward the house.

Wilson put his hand up and shook his head. "Uh-uh, no way."

She gave him a pretentious, shocked expression. "What do you mean? I'm a member of the press; I've got rights."

"Out here, you're a member of the press. Over there, you're a trespasser, interfering with an ongoing investigation, possibly tampering with evidence. Probably something worse. I'm sure I'll think of something."

"This is ridiculous," she protested. "The public has a right to…."

His laughter cut her off. Her mouth snapped shut. She was starting to look offended, but Wilson didn't seem to care much.

"I don't see what's so funny."

"You," he said. "You're hilarious. I can't believe you're going to try to play that card. As if you give a damn about the public's right to anything."

"What's that supposed to mean?" she demanded.

"It means I'm not some rookie. You seem to forget that I know you, Gloria. The only thing you care about is *your* name. On the front page. Above the fold."

"Jesus, Charlie," she said, "when did you get so cynical?"

"I don't know, Glor. I guess about the time my job description started, *including talking to reporters*, I guess."

3

Coroner's Office

Two hours after Wilson's head hit his pillow, he was startled out of his sleep by what sounded like a fire alarm going off in his bedroom. Somehow, his mind jumped to the conclusion that the building was ablaze, and he jumped from his bed to find his cell phone ringing on his nightstand. Blearily, he looked at the clock. Big, red block letters told him it was just 4:30 in the morning. Given the hour, Wilson knew the call must be for something important.

"Wilson here," he mumbled into the phone, still half asleep.

"Hey, it's Mark Wallace from the coroner's headquarters office. I know you had a late night, but we have some results from the Aricksons' autopsies, and I thought you'd want to hear what we found."

Wilson's eyes shot open. "What, already? Usually, I'm on your ass for days or weeks to get my results."

"What do you want me to say? This is Steven Arickson and his whole family. I have everybody on me to get this done."

"Everybody? Like whom?" Wilson inquired curiously.

"Everybody on my team. Turns out, one of the richest men in the world is considered more important than the mystery of the rotting meth head. You're the primary on this case, right?"

"Yeah, I am," Wilson replied.

Wallace gave a dark chuckle. "Well, good luck with that. All the big boys are on high alert."

"Great," Wilson muttered. "Thanks for the heads-up."

"Not a problem. Are you coming down, or what?"

"Yeah, I'll be there as soon as I can."

Wilson grabbed his shirt off the bedroom floor while his other hand searched for his cigarettes. He took a couple of drags as he headed for the bathroom. He showered, slid into a sleek Calvin Klein suit, and stood in front of the bathroom mirror, studying himself for a moment. Wilson stood right at six feet and had kept his muscle tone from his college football days when he played for a little Division II college out in Wyoming. He was a star athlete but never cared too much about making football a career. He came from a family of detectives, and it had been his dream to become one for as long as he could remember.

However, now, as his intense green eyes stared into themselves, he wondered, *who am I? What am I doing with my life? I've got no family, no friends — it's all just dead bodies and crime scenes.*

Wilson tried to keep himself busy as a distraction from his empty life, but he couldn't avoid the intrusive thoughts every time. He shook his head, sprayed on some cologne, and headed out, leaving his existential crisis in the bathroom, floating in a cloud of Acqua Di Gio.

Wilson stopped at his favorite coffee shop on the ground floor of his high-rise apartment and picked up his usual large coffee loaded with sugar. He smiled at Jess, his regular barista, a bubbly blonde with a nose piercing and cat eyes. He always tried flirting with her but never worked up the nerve to ask her out. She winked at him, handing him his coffee, her fingers lightly brushing against his during the exchange. Wilson hesitated as he considered asking her to dinner but then remembered the Aricksons' corpses were waiting for him. He bid her goodbye and took off without a word.

He consoled himself by saying, *She's probably not my type, anyway*. If Charles was going to settle down, he needed a woman who understood his line of work. He had a woman just like that in mind, but he had not yet made a move.

He made it to the coroner's office before rush hour. The office was an enormous, archaic building that looked like it had been an asylum at some point in its history. It was a giant cinder-block building painted entirely white. Apart from two rusted metal rails on the west side leading up to the main entrance steps and two large metal doors on either side of the building, nothing broke the monotony of dullness. The enormous, dreary structure gave Wilson a queasy stomach every time he looked at it. He was sure that mad doctors had experimented on patients and then dissected them in the building at some point or another.

Wilson ran into Wallace at the top of the stairs when he arrived. He looked just like a guy would expect a coroner to look, with ash-colored skin and deep-set eyes that were grayish blue under his bottom lashes. As ghostly as Mark's appearance was, Wilson always liked him. He had chosen a strange profession, but he was a likable guy who was good at what he did. As a homicide detective, Wilson could hardly judge a man's line of work anyway.

"Hey, detective!" Wallace called out. "I can't say it's nice to see you here."

"I understand. I wish it were on better terms. It's horrible what happened, isn't it?" Wilson said.

"One of the worst I've ever seen," Mark agreed. "Whoever did this is demented."

They walked down the empty halls that glowed pale yellow from the fluorescent light and smelled of formaldehyde and industrial-strength cleaner. It felt like a combination of a science lab and a hospital. The nauseating smells of death mixed with Wilson's expensive cologne confused the olfactory senses — gore and glamour mingled in an unlikely dance down the hall.

The two came to the end of the hallway and entered the morgue. Wilson's eyes fell on the stainless-steel drawers containing the dead bodies. There was a stainless-steel table in the middle of the room with an operating light hovering above it and a drain underneath it. Wilson put his back against one of the metal drawer walls as Mark pulled out the five drawers that held the bodies of the Aricksons.

"You ready to do this?" Mark asked.

"Ready as I'll ever be," he answered, stepping over to stand beside the pale coroner.

"All right. Well, first off, the strangulation marks on their necks suggest a struggle," Mark explained as he slid a finger along the bruised neck of Lisa Anne.

Wilson nodded and leaned in to get a good look at the deceased supermodel's bruised neck.

"But here's the weird thing," Mark continued. "They didn't die of suffocation. The killer started to strangle by the looks of it and then changed his mind."

"How can you tell that?"

"Well, for one, the trachea isn't damaged enough. Also, the bruising isn't deep the way it would be if that was the intention."

Wilson nodded, wondering if the supermodel had taken the killer by surprise. There would've been a skirmish, leading to strangulation and the eventual cause of death.

Wallace then moved to Trey Arickson's corpse.

"Which brings me to these slashes all over all their bodies. You see the way the skin peels off here?" he said, pointing to a deep laceration in Trey's thigh.

Wilson nodded, examining the gash on the would-be NFL star.

"So, I can assume that it was most likely a large knife that caused this — not a machete or anything in that range — more like a kitchen knife that you might use to cut up meat or slice pizza or something."

"You've officially ruined meat *and* pizza for me, Mark. Please, no more food references."

"How come? Feeling too squeamish? Queasy? Wanna take a breather for a second?" The eccentric coroner replied with a sly grin.

"No problem. Go on," Wilson said.

"So, the lacerations caused by the knife led to a significant amount of blood loss, causing their untimely demise. These people were dead before they were hung," Mark announced.

"How did the perp manage to hang them all from a fifteen-foot-high ceiling with nooses?" Wilson wondered aloud. "It was a chore for us to get them down, even with five of us there."

The fact that the killer went through the trouble of hanging them means that the motive was personal.

"There's more," Mark said. "The toxicology screen shows they were all drugged. We found traces of heroin in each of the bodies."

Wilson frowned at that. Why would the killer use heroin as his drug of choice? That fact makes the case even more troubling.

Wilson said after a brief pause, "So, let me quickly go through this to make sure I got it. The killer started to strangle the victims but decided against that and went to hack away with a kitchen knife on the family, and *after* they bled to death, he strung them up in that old house. Where do the drugs fit into all this?"

"I have no clue, but that about covers it," Mark replied, glancing down at Lisa Anne's body. "I don't know if this is helpful to you, but strangulation marks appear only on adults. The three kids have trauma to their necks from being hung."

That made it even more interesting, and it threw Wilson's theory of the killer being taken by surprise by the supermodel out the window. The fact that the kids weren't strangled suggested that the killer didn't want them to suffer. Maybe that's why he first strangled the adults before hacking away at them.

"Looks like I have my work cut out for me. Thanks again, Mark. Hopefully, I won't have to see you anytime soon if it means I'm coming to this place."

"I hear that a lot," Mark said, staring at Lisa Anne's face.

Wilson turned to leave the morgue when Mark called out to him.

"Do you think it had anything to do with the problems they'd been having?"

"What's that?" Wilson stopped on his heels and turned around to face the coroner.

"I heard he was thinking of calling it quits with her. To be honest, I was shocked when I heard that because he's loaded, but Lisa Anne was still out of his league."

"How do you know that?"

"It was all over the tabloids."

Wilson frowned.

"A guy has to do something to pass the time in this place," Mark shrugged.

"And you believe what the tabloids say?" Wilson asked, dismissing the coroner's comment.

"There were a few photos of him with another woman."

"You ever heard of Photoshop, Mark?"

"Of course, but these appeared to look genuine."

"Isn't that the whole point?"

"I guess so," Mark answered, feeling a little sheepish for sharing tabloid gossip with a detective who worked with factual evidence.

Mark was saved from the embarrassment of continuing the conversation when Wilson's cell phone vibrated in his pocket.

"This is Wilson."

"Wilson, it's Aaron."

"I was just leaving the coroner's office, Chief. It seems like this is going to be a bit more complicated than I thought."

"You bet your ass it is," the Chief retorted.

"So, have you already spoken with Mark?" Wilson was perplexed by the Chief's curt response.

"Nope. I don't have a clue what that creepy body jabber found out. I'm out here at the house right now, and it looks like we're onto something. Book it out here, got it?"

"Yes, sir."

"This is big, Wilson."

4

The Suspects

The flimsy yellow police tape gleamed under the dark clouds gathering atop, adding to the foreboding vibe around the property. Wilson was secretly glad for the squad cars swarming the property. He didn't like the idea of roaming around alone at the crime scene. The property seemed quite different from what it had been the night before. Even if it weren't for the ominous vibes surrounding the house, Wilson still wouldn't want to be there alone, given what the house had witnessed. The gruesome image of the mutilated family hanging in the candlelight's glow was etched into his brain, and he knew it would haunt him for years to come. Glumly, he accepted the trauma, sweeping it under the rug for now, along with a myriad of memories he wanted to forget. From afar, he saw officer Cooper jogging toward him.

"Good thing you're here, Detective. The forensic team pulled partial prints from the scene and succeeded in matching them to a possible suspect," Cooper said, panting heavily.

Sometimes, Wilson feared for the future of the police department. Cooper opened his mouth to speak, but Wilson just couldn't resist.

"Maybe you should catch your breath first."

"We found two sets of fingerprints," Cooper said, ignoring Wilson's comment. "One set on the picture frame and the other on the nylon ropes used to hang the bodies."

"And the suspect?" Wilson asked, remembering that the team was able to match the partial print.

"The print on the picture frame belongs to Mr. Arickson's former assistant, Declan Herring," Cooper replied. "I dug around a bit and found that he's the real inventor of the Fireburner software. It was his idea; he came up with the concept."

Wilson frowned, recalling Mr. Arickson as the company's owner, "He wasn't part of the company?"

Cooper shook his head. "Turns out, Steven Arickson financed Herring's idea from the get-go," Cooper explained. "Herring came up with the concept and developed it with Arickson, but since Arickson had financed the entire thing, his claim to the software outweighed Herring's. He left Herring in the dust once the software was completed and didn't give him any credit. Herring even tried taking Arickson to court a couple of times, but that was an exercise in futility. If he'd had the money to fund a court battle, he'd probably have developed the idea on his own," Cooper said, shaking his head sadly.

"That makes sense," Wilson said, nodding.

"Herring attacked Arickson once — years ago — and that's what put his fingerprints in the system in the first place for aggravated assault."

“The second set?” Wilson inquired.

“That belongs to the original designer of the software, Michael Smith, a designer and engineer.”

“That’s interesting,” Wilson said, frowning.

The execution style and mutilation made it seem like the killer had a personal reason. Wilson didn’t think anyone would go to such an extent over stolen software, but then again, Steven Arickson had made a fortune with that software, which just made him wealthier. For someone to happen upon an idea worth that much and lose it to some power-hungry bastard could very well break them.

“Hopefully, the case just got slightly less complicated,” he added in an undertone, wondering how beneficial his success, in this case, could be. “Let’s go meet the Chief.”

Wilson walked toward the house for another round of the heinous crime scene with Cooper, still marveling at the depths some people sank to. He found this case fascinating. Despite having years of experience under his belt, he’d never come across anything like this.

His train of thought was interrupted by the Chief calling out to him from the patio. Wilson nodded and started walking briskly toward the Chief.

Wilson stepped onto the patio, and a light rain began to fall as if on cue.

Great, Wilson thought. *Just what I was missing.*

Wilson didn't want to be here in the first place, and his uneasiness increased with God going the extra mile to make it scarier for him.

So much for less ominous.

Finding his resolve, he walked up the front steps and crossed the porch where the bodies of the Arickson family had been lined up just the night before. He waited for the Chief as he finished talking to a couple of officers. The fact that the boss was taking such an active role reminded him of the importance of this case.

"I'm here, Chief," he called. "Cooper briefed me on Herring and Smith."

Just as the Chief replied, the entrance of Detective Cassidy Stewart diverted Wilson's attention. From somewhere far off in the distance, Wilson could hear the Chief speaking, but his words had just lost all meaning. Stewart was not what you pictured when you thought of a detective; she looked more like a swimsuit model than an officer of the law. She was built like a gymnast, except for the fact that she was busty. She had honey-colored hair that went down to the middle of her back, but she kept it pulled back in a ponytail during office hours. Cassidy looked like a college cheerleader when she showed up at crime scenes, but Wilson knew her well enough by now to know that that was just the tip of the iceberg. Stewart was as tough as nails and could out-sleuth anyone on the force. He'd noticed people tended not to take her seriously when they first met her. They wouldn't have made that mistake if they had gotten a chance to meet her a second time.

"Do we have any leads on where these two could be?" Cassidy asked as she stood behind Wilson, catching him a little off guard.

"Not yet," the Chief answered. "Stewart is the one who worked the evidence and sourced the leads," the Chief added with a sly glance at Wilson.

Alright then.

"Nice work, Stewart," Wilson said, turning to face his gorgeous colleague.

When their eyes met, Wilson felt his bottom half tingle for a split second, and his pulse slightly quickened. His lips automatically curved into a faint smile. He knew that Stewart was a sharp enough detective that she probably noticed his pupils swell — a sign of arousal for most people.

Quickly finding his composure, he added, "But let's start at Herring's residence."

"What about Michael?" Cooper asked, stepping between the two.

Cooper could feel the sexual tension from where he was standing, and jealousy pricked his insides. He had known Stewart for a long time — long before either of them joined the force. He had a major crush on her ever since the first time he saw her back in high school. Even though he didn't like admitting it, Stewart was partly the reason he joined the force in the first place. He'd been content enough running his family's deli for years, but he'd realized that being a deli manager wouldn't get him a girl like Cassidy Stewart. So, he decided to attend the police academy and graduated with top honors, with his specialty being homicide, to get closer to his high school crush.

The exchange between his crush and Wilson made it clear that he had competition. Deep down, Cooper didn't like his odds. Wilson was tall, toned, and looked like he had stepped out of a Ralph Lauren ad most days. Cooper, on the other hand, was built like a horse jockey, with carrot-colored hair and an awkward sense of humor. He knew he didn't stand a chance against Wilson. Wilson was a *Magnum, P.I.* kind of cop, and Cooper was closer to Barney Fife.

"We'll get to him, too," Wilson answered. "I want to hit Herring first, though. He had stronger ties and a bigger reason to knock off Steven Arickson and the aggravated assault, of course."

"Keep tabs on both of them," the Chief said. "This case made the news. Put out an APB for them, put them on the no-fly list — basically, any way out of this city should be on high alert for both. They're packing their bags right now if they aren't already out of the city."

"We'll get warrants for both of them," Wilson assured the Chief.

"You need me to tag along?" Cooper offered.

"I think two is enough," Stewart said before Wilson could answer.

"I guess I'll stay here and look for more evidence then," Officer Cooper said, unable to mask his scowl at Wilson.

"We'll be back for an update on anything you find after we talk to Mr. Herring," Wilson told the disgruntled newbie. "Richard is on his way, so he can help out while we make a house call."

Cooper murmured, "Sure."

"You ready then?" Stewart asked as she elbowed Wilson in the ribs.

He was flustered again by the exchange, but he shook it off and answered, "Ready as I'll ever be."

"Let's hope," Cooper grumbled as the two walked away.

"You can call in the warrant on the way," Wilson said as the two walked down the driveway and climbed into his squad car. "I'd say we have enough to get one immediately."

5

The Suspects' Residences

Wilson's wristwatch ticked away as he stared ahead at the lazy street. He was waiting for his partner to return from the brief break they'd taken to get something to eat. The job was tough; as it turns out, chasing a murder suspect on an empty stomach sucks. To their credit, though, they were hurrying the process as fast as possible, going to their regular *Shawarma* guy who'd serve them first.

Wilson mentally ticked off the checklist in his head — he had everything he needed to conduct a search. Getting anxious, he honked his horn to tell Stewart to hurry up.

"Gimme a minute!" Stewart yelled from across the street. "YOU KNOW! THESE THINGS DON'T COOK THEMSELVES!"

Wilson glanced at the guy as a bead of sweat formed on his forehead as a hot sauce bottle slipped from his hand. He caught it midway and hurriedly apologized as he completed the *shawarma* and handed it off to Stewart, who jogged back to the car, yelling, "Go! Go! Go!"

Wilson calmly pulled off into the street as Stewart sat back in the car.

"You didn't have to do that, you know," Wilson said as he drove to the perp's address.

"What?!" Stewart asked innocently. "I mean, look at this perfection. This is life, eh? Shawarma and a murder chase."

Wilson gave Stewart a sideways glance. "Yeah, that's not going to work. And you, you shrew! I'm the regular here. I don't want my guy to fear me!"

"What's going to happen if he's scared of you?"

Wilson thought about it for a moment and said, "Shawarmas made under duress just don't taste right."

Stewart laughed out loud at that, unable to come up with a reply to it. So, she pulled out the wrapped Levantine delicacy, handed one to her partner, and ate the other herself.

"I bought a third one, too," Stewart said casually.

Wilson frowned. "For Herring?"

"As a matter of fact, yeah!" Stewart said through a mouthful of food. "I thought we'd play the good cops for a while. If that doesn't work, I'll at least be happy knowing he ate something with my spit in it."

Wilson nodded, "The bastard made life a living hell. The media's already sniffing around, and these ass hats don't miss a shot to defame us!"

"Woah there, Wilson!" Stewart said. "Nothing they print is technically incorrect, you know. You aren't going to tell me our media broadcasts are fiction."

Wilson glanced at Stewart, knowing very well that this was his attempt at passing the time till they reached Herring's place, which wasn't that far away.

"I'm telling the Chief you said that." Wilson bit off a large piece to chew and slowly chewed away, choosing to spend the rest of his ride enjoying the shawarma instead of catering to Stewart's antics.

Stewart pulled a face and decided to focus on her food as well. They had gradually moved from the place downtown, near their precinct, to a rather seldom traveled part of town.

It wasn't quite as nice as where Arickson lived, but it was far superior to where the average cop spent his time. A crime that takes place in places like this is on a whole different level — a level way above the pay grade of a normal cop.

"Jesus, you live in a place like this and get booked for a couple of murders… he'll get bullied for the rest of his life by his friends," Wilson said. "I mean, at least, get caught for defrauding the IRS or something, right?"

Stewart snorted, having just taken a sip of water. Suddenly, she pointed toward the right, indicating the turn. Wilson cut right and pulled up to a quaint street, which seemed like a heavenly place to live.

***

Stewart peered out the window at the enormous Victorian home at the back of perfectly manicured lawns.

Still trying to understand the level of wealth one must accumulate to live in a place like this, Wilson said, "Jesus, psychopaths don't always come from the hood, do they? Who knew money was the root of all evil?"

Stewart chuckled, "You know, you should write that down."

The two took in the sights as they pulled into the long-paved driveway that led back to Declan Herring's residence — a two-story Eastlake-style Victorian that was a cream color with pink trim along the roof. The house had small balconies and patios everywhere and a turret that made it look as much like a castle as a home.

"Jesus, no wonder Herring killed Arickson. Imagine having the greatest idea you ever had stolen and living in a place like this," Stewart said, looking appalled. "I'd be in a pretty stabby mood myself, I tell you."

Wilson pulled up to the house to find the first sign that they'd missed their target: the gate was open. Stewart and Wilson exchanged a glance, and Wilson gunned it for the house. Stewart got a glimpse of the twenty-foot-high iron gate that had a giant *A* on it and felt a twinge of wonderment at God for giving so much to people who were just so damn stupid. Wilson pulled up to the circular driveway with a swan fountain built around the middle.

"Jesus Christ, really?" Stewart exclaimed, unable to hold back her shock at someone stupid enough to commit murder when they had a lavish life.

The two of them got out of the car and went separate ways toward the house. While Detective Wilson walked discreetly up the front steps of the house, Stewart went around back to cover the perimeter of the enormous estate. The partners had an understanding and worked in sync together, with her covering the back entrance in case Herring tried to flee. Even as she ran along the perimeter, she saw the rat bastard had built multiple entry and exit points, and knowing the kind of dough these people had, all of them were probably secure.

Stewart hung back about fifty yards so that she had a panoramic view of the rear of the large house, clutching her pistol, waiting, and watching.

On the other side of the large mansion, Wilson grabbed the antique doorknob and turned it, but it was locked. He frowned, wondering why Herring would even bother locking the front door if he were going to leave the main gate open. He banged his fist on the door, giving the heavy oak piece four serious thuds. Wilson stood there, thinking over the best plan of action. He strained to hear any noise from within, but the place seemed silent. He couldn't see inside the property because of the expensive mosaic glass windows. Not wanting to give Herring any more time to escape than he already had, Wilson drew his department-issued piece and stepped back, letting two shots fly off at either of the hinges.

"Wilson!" Stewart's voice crackled over the radio. "Wilson, come in! Over!" she yelled, knowing there was no point in keeping things quiet — not that they were particularly quiet when they barreled up the driveway.

"I needed to open the door… and if the backup wasn't on its way, it is now. Over."

"Wow, smart ass. Over and out."

Wilson busted the door open, his gun pointed straight ahead, looking for Herring.

"Declan, are you here?" Wilson called. "If you don't want to leave here in a body bag, you'd better show yourself, hands in the air."

Wilson took a quick look around the house. Room by room, the detective stayed close to the walls, following the barrel of his gun as he checked for any sign of the suspect. By the looks of the place, Mr. Herring had already packed up and left in a hurry. The house was in such disarray that it looked as if a wrestling match had taken place. In the office, papers were strewn all over the floor, and the sheets and comforter were ripped from the bed in the master bedroom. The kitchen was trashed, and a lot of the furniture looked out of order. Wilson noticed that even a couple of pictures were knocked off the walls in the hall.

"It's all clear!" Wilson said on the radio.

He started going through the mess, but it all seemed like papers that had nothing to do with anything they could use right now. There were a couple of research papers on the latest advancements in his field.

"We need to get our forensics team out here to get his computers and get records on his cell phone ASAP," Wilson said as Stewart approached. "They might be able to pull something from this mess."

"Okay, I'll go call it in," Stewart replied, taking one last look at the room before she jogged out.

Wilson, meanwhile, continued searching the property in the best way he could, looking for any possible clue that might lead him to Herring. This guy was good because he certainly didn't leave any traces behind. A couple of minutes later, Stewart joined him, and they searched the place for a good twenty minutes before the teams arrived. Wilson handed the crime scene to the officer leading the forensics team and gestured for Stewart to follow him.

"Let's go to the Smiths' house," Wilson suggested. "There's no use in hanging around here wasting time."

The two of them walked out, and Wilson's day suddenly took a turn for the worse, and it already wasn't going too well. There, leaning against the hood of his car, smoking a cigarette, was the woman who was the reason for his deep distaste for the media.

Biting back half a dozen curses, Wilson turned to Stewart. “Do not stop walking, or I swear to God…!” Wilson left the sentence hanging, and Stewart nodded solemnly.

“Yeah, calm down, dude. You don’t need to throw a temper tantrum.”

Wilson shook his head and walked toward his car, and the vulture, in the form of a five-foot-two, perky, but dead-smart blonde journalist named Marquez was already approaching him on the patio. Ignoring her completely, Wilson started walking toward his car.

“I could have told you that Herring fled, you know. I don’t get why you continue not trusting me!”

“Ohh!” Wilson said derisively. “You know damn well why I distrust you!”

“Why?” Marquez asked. “Is it because of that damn OT story again?”

Wilson paused for a moment to turn around, and Stewart immediately tried to keep him walking by dragging him along. However, Wilson stood his ground.

“You came up to me and interviewed me in good faith, saying that you wanted to write a good piece about the police department. You then went behind my back and misquoted me in the entire article," Wilson said, his eyes deadlocked with Marquez.

"Call that a professional wake-up call, Wilson," Marquez said. "It's the world, buddy. Get over it."

"I'll get over your mo-"

"Woah-ho-ho!" Cassidy Stewart had to step in instantly. "Really think you wanna say that to a journalist, buddy?"

Wilson stopped in his tracks. Something in Stewart's eyes got through to him, and he knew anything he said after that was just going to be a liability. It took an enormous amount of self-restraint, but he eventually got a hold of himself. He was about to walk off when Marquez called out from behind them.

"Hey Wilson, tell me you're at least hitting that for her to have that much control over you."

That was the limit. Wilson knew he should've kept walking, but he just had to turn around and get in that last remark.

"Hey, Marquez, how about this for the record?" Wilson began, shaking himself free of Stewart's grasp, turning around to face the journalist. "You are a wily, scummy piece of…"

"Alrighty, we're going back to the car!" Stewart said, grasping his arm and pulling him away from Marquez.

"That's the bullshit you wanna talk about instead of the fact that a journalist knows something she isn't supposed to know?" Stewart said, her mouth hanging open.

"What the hell do you want me to do about it? Make her unknow it?!" Wilson snapped. "And you! It's that damn OT story! You know what shit you pulled!" Turning around for one last jab at the scathing journalist.

Marquez sighed audibly, shutting her eyes tight. "Look, boomer! I know you think I hosed you guys with that OT story, and I've been out in the weeds ever since. But here's the thing — that story wasn't about the entire department, and you know it. You know the guys I was after on that one — the highfliers. Do you know how much those guys game the system for? During a recession, when city revenues are way down, and we're paying an awful amount of money for guys to direct traffic in their off-hours? Somebody was writing that story, and I could have been a lot harder on everybody. But, okay, let's say I was the asshole on that one. Fine. It doesn't change the fact that I'm the one who's got to work in this town at the end of the day. The hitters coming in from all over — and I promise they're filling up the hotel rooms right now — they've got no such loyalties. They will burn your whole department down just because they like the pretty colors. You think I'm lying about that?"

Wilson paused at that. He didn't want to believe her, but he just couldn't bring himself to admit that she made sense.

"It's too damn bad. The jig is up, Detective. The chaos has officially begun, whether you know it or not. One of the biggest names in this country is dead in your yard. This is not ending well for you as far as the coverage is concerned. Not unless you already have a guy in custody. Preferably an Al-Qaeda member — that would focus people's attention on something else."

Wilson shook his head at that, "I knew talking to you was useless!" He was just about to sit in his car when Marquez blocked his way.

"You will need an ally here!"

Wilson laughed. "And you're going to convince me you're that ally?"

Marquez pulled a card from her pocket and shoved it into his hand.

"Look, I know you've got your reasons for hating me. I get that, but you know I'm right. You also know that I'm not a bad person. I called it as I saw it, and if that doesn't sit well with you, you're not the cop who should be working on a case like this. Because you won't be any better than them."

Marquez turned around and walked off, not even giving him a chance to say anything.

Wilson and Stewart watched the house for a moment before ducking into the car and grabbing the radio.

"You know, Stewart, one of these days, I'm gonna pop a cap in Herring's ass for all the trouble this guy has caused me," Wilson said, staring at the house in dismay.

He didn't let it on, but the stress of the case was getting to him — piece by piece.

"Hey, get in line. You'll have to wrestle the gun out of my hands." Stewart's attempt at comedy was a welcome change of pace from the seriousness of it all.

The two detectives sat in the car. Wilson absentmindedly put the keys in the ignition when his car radio flared up.

"Detective Wilson? Are you there? Laura here; over."

"Just got in the car," Wilson answered Laura's call over the radio. "Declan Herring's house was a bust."

"You didn't find him?" Laura asked, sounding disappointed.

Wilson pulled a face. "I'm sorry, I guess? I'll try to do a better job the next time around."

"Well, you're in luck. I have the address for Michael Smith's place in front of me," Laura said in a tone. "Over."

Wilson paused for a second, almost certain of what was coming now. "Would you be ever so kind as to send me the address? Over," Wilson spoke slowly, choosing his words very carefully.

There was a pause on the phone line as Wilson waited anxiously.

"Sending it on your phone, killjoy," Laura said glumly.

It seemed like this was one of the rare wins for Wilson, who rarely got the better of Laura in one of their verbal exchanges.

"Although, now that I think about it, I also seem to have some other information related to the wife," Laura added nonchalantly.

"What are you talking about?" Wilson asked instantly, then clapped his hand on his forehead, facepalming himself.

"What are the magic words?" Laura said, the glee in her voice transmitting over the radio.

"Please..." the word came out from somewhere between the gritted teeth.

"Gotcha! Sending the details to your phone now. Don't bother me again. Over and out." The line went dead.

"...You're the one who called me," Wilson said faintly to no one in particular.

"Yea," Stewart scoffed, "you aren't into each other."

Wilson was about to come up with a scathing remark about Stewart's workaholic lifestyle when he realized she probably got more date offers in a week than he would. She was downright drop-dead gorgeous. He was about to say it when his phone binged. Somehow, Laura had gotten the better of him even when she wasn't here. The timing was impeccable.

"Saved by the bell, Stewart, saved by the bell," Wilson said, picking up his phone and going over the texts from Laura.

"It looks like Michael's wife, Susan, wants to file a missing person's report. According to her, Michael left to meet someone after a strange phone call and never came back."

"Is she at her house now?" Stewart asked, her interest piqued.

"Fucking Laura!" Wilson laughed, shaking his head. "She is somehow always in the right place at the right time. Susan was literally on the call with Laura about ten minutes ago. She asked her to wait there and told her that a couple of officers would be there to take her statement."

Stewart was visibly impressed, which was weird considering that Wilson had rarely seen her impressed at anything. "She's smart," Stewart said appreciatively. "It's good that she has a thing for you, you know. Who knows how else you'll make do?!"

Wilson turned to face Stewart slowly, "You know… sometimes, you just take shots for no reason whatsoever… what was the purpose of that?"

"Bitch isn't a good color on you, Wilson," Stewart said casually. "How far is the Smith residence?"

Wilson paused for a second, then said, "It is a good color on you, though."

He turned the car's ignition on, and the engine revved to life.

"It's about fifteen miles away."

Before Stewart could get in the last word, Wilson gunned the engine, drowning her out.

The GPS calculated the fastest way there, and Wilson ripped through Wine Valley toward the second suspect's home. There was no need to hurry since Laura had already ensured that Susan wasn't going anywhere — but then again, this line of work had often taught him not to take time for granted. A single second could mean the difference between life and death, and people who understand this have usually made the mistake of thinking they have the freedom of time.

The few squad cars that accompanied them were having a little difficulty keeping up with them, which somehow uplifted the melancholy mood that Wilson had gotten into. The fiery duo kept up the pace until they screeched to a halt right in front of Smith's residence.

"Subtlety isn't your strong suit, is it?" Stewart said, hopping out of the car, pretending the world was spinning underneath her.

"You know, Stewart, the person least likely to run is the one reporting the crime. And the person most likely to have conducted the killing — at least in most cases — is the one who reported the crime," Wilson smiled. "Don't worry. She ain't going nowhere!"

The squad cars reached the destination a good half-minute after Wilson did.

"Hey detective, you know, I was this close to pulling you over," one of the fresh recruits said, holding up his thumb and index finger at Wilson as he got out of the car with his mentor. "But damn, that was fun!"

Wilson slowly turned around to stare at the kid. Just then, his mentor, an older officer in his early thirties, threw a bag of donuts at him.

"Jesus Christ, Eric!" he exclaimed. "WHAT WAS THE FIRST RULE?!"

"Shut up and listen," Eric said in the smallest voice.

"So, shut up and listen!" the officer yelled, giving Wilson an embarrassing side glance. "Apologies, detective. I swear these recruits get worse year after year."

"Why don't you guys wait here?" Wilson said, posing it as a question, but his face made it clear it was an order.

Wilson shook his head and turned to the house — set on a massive grassy lot lined with perfectly sculpted hedges and dotted with citrus trees. The house itself was solid mirrored glass on the front side, which was as long as a football field. Two big ceramic statues graced the entrance to the home.

"What do you think about the house?"

"It's ridiculous. What on God's green earth are you gonna do with a house this big?"

"I suppose crime takes up quite a bit of space," Stewart said, walking toward the main gate leading into the house.

The detectives arrived at a long concrete wall. A Spartan steel gate stretched across the driveway. Like the rest of the house, it looked like a work of art from a science fiction film. Wilson spotted the buzzer on a stand beside the driveway. He hit the button and waited.

Finally, a tentative reply— which Wilson assumed was from Susan Smith — cut through the static, "H… hello?"

"Detective Wilson and Detective Stewart, Mrs. Smith."

"Why the hell did you say my name second?" Stewart whispered.

"Oh, thank God!"

The voice seemed to change in an instant as if the woman finally took a long-awaited sigh of relief.

"Come in. Please, come in."

They heard a buzzer sound, and the gate began to slide smoothly into the wall.

"Alrighty then."

The detectives exchanged looks as Wilson maneuvered the car through the entrance and toward the house. Wilson pulled up the driveway and saw Mrs. Smith waiting on the porch to greet them.

"Oh, thank God you're here!" Mrs. Smith said, almost running toward Wilson as if he were her knight in shining armor. Thankfully, she stopped short of the detectives and grasped their hands as if she were drowning and they were the life raft.

Just then, it hit Wilson. The poor girl was under the impression that the detectives had arrived to assist her husband; she had no idea that her husband was a suspect in a heinous homicide.

Wilson pulled his best poker face as he contemplated how he wanted to play this. Wilson could see that the woman was going through a rough patch. Her hair was messy as if she'd just rolled out of bed, her clothes were wrinkled, and she bore the unmistakable aura of someone who was one accidental broken glass away from completely giving up on herself.

“Thank God you are here,” she said, with tears gathering at the corners of her drooping, bloodshot eyes. “I didn’t think anyone would do anything until forty-eight hours had passed.”

“Mrs. Smith,” Stewart said, taking a step toward the exhausted woman.

Instinctively, Wilson knew what was going to come out of her mouth, and he also knew that there was no way he would be able to stop it.

“Your husband is a suspect in a homicide case. We have reason to believe that he has skipped town.”

Wilson bowed his head, rubbing his forehead subtly. Internally, he prepped himself for the emotional shitstorm that was about to follow. He gave Stewart an annoyed look — that was the moment Stewart realized that she might have spoken out of turn.

“That can’t be,” Susan Smith countered, shaking her head as she took a couple of steps back into her house. “Michael would never….”

“We have prints, Mrs. Smith,” Wilson told her, taking charge of the situation. “They came from the crime scene.”

“This makes no sense. He doesn’t even litter. He is compassionate. Michael’s never been in trouble in his life. He….”

"It was Steven Arickson and his family," Wilson interrupted her. "The man who made billions from your husband's design."

He was trying his best to get the ball rolling. He'd spent enough time interrogating distraught spouses to know they loved wasting time.

"Michael let that go a long time ago. We've done fine without my husband getting the credit he deserved for his work on the Fireburner project. He's had plenty of success. He would never do something like that for money, revenge, or whatever you think he did it for. We have a baby on the way. He would never have…." Susan suddenly collapsed onto the floor of the entryway.

Wilson accidentally audibly sighed, earning a hard elbow to the ribs from Stewart.

"Drama queen…" Wilson mouthed to Stewart, looking at the crumpled figure sobbing on the floor.

"I am so sorry, Mrs. Smith," Stewart said.

Meanwhile, Wilson remained quiet, his gaze affixed on the hysterical woman.

"Why don't we go into the living room, where we can ask you some questions?" she suggested, helping the distraught Mrs. Smith from the floor.

When Susan had composed herself, the three went into the family room. Wilson pulled a recorder from his pocket, set it on the coffee table, and began to ask questions. Susan was still in shock, but she cooperated with the detectives. As she answered each of their questions, she insisted that there was some mistake and that the detectives had the wrong person. There was no way that her husband could have been involved in such a heinous act.

"In cases like these, family members are always completely caught off guard," Stewart explained.

"Steven wanted to start a family… He would never…. We have tried for five years to get pregnant, though," Susan told them. "We have never been happier. This makes no sense."

"I know this is a lot to take in, but try to listen to my questions and answer them as accurately as possible. If something else is happening, you may be able to lead us to it, but we need to know exactly what has been happening; every detail matters right now."

Wilson often used this technique to get loved ones who were in denial to talk. He knew that if Susan thought that her information could help vindicate her husband, whom she was positive was innocent, then she'd calm down enough to provide some information that might help lead to her fugitive husband.

"Have you noticed your husband acting strange lately?" Stewart asked.

"I guess a little, but we just found out about the baby, so I figured he was just nervous about becoming a dad and getting used to that idea."

"What had he been doing that was out of the ordinary?"

"The only thing I noticed was that he seemed worried all the time."

Guilty conscience, perhaps, Wilson thought as he jotted down notes. "We recently also had a break-in, which seemed to set him on edge."

"A break-in?" Wilson asked. "In the home?"

"They just got into the garage — probably just teenagers looking to see what they could snag and run away with. The alarm scared them off before they could get anything of value, though. They just grabbed a few worthless things lying around the garage and left. Michael was beside himself about it, though. That is how he is — he doesn't understand people who steal."

"What about the night he left?" Stewart asked.

"He just said that he had to meet someone for work. He didn't say who it was. But he meets people for work all the time, so there was nothing unusual about it."

"Did you notice if any of his belongings were missing? Clothes that he may have packed?" Wilson asked.

"No."

"Does Michael have a credit card you don't see the activity on?"

"He has a couple, I guess, for work things. Why?"

"We will need to check his records for ticket purchases."

"He would not just leave his family," Susan insisted.

"Thank you for your time," Detective Stewart said as she got up.

Wilson said the same, and the two took off for the Aricksons' home. On the way, Detective Wilson informed Laura that he needed the suspects' credit cards, phone numbers, and e-mail addresses to be run immediately.

6

The Arickson Residence

ou know, sometimes… there's something so despicable about humanity that you just can't come to terms with it."

Wilson looked out of the window, driving toward the Arickson estate just outside of town on a rolling vineyard.

"She's a victim too in all this. If not for her, then for his unborn child. If not for it, then at least for himself… the bastard had all the reasons in the world not to do it, but he still did it. No matter how many times you see it in this line of work… it still chips away at you."

Stewart said nothing of that. She was having a tough time coming to terms with it herself.

"Do you think he could've had a shot at the Fireburner fortunes by executing the biggest thorn in his side?" Stewart asked suddenly, "It's not like he needed the extra money… but you can never discount greed from the equation."

"Huh…" Wilson thoughtfully wondered if that could serve as the motive behind the murders. "We won't know unless we catch him."

The radio crackled to life, "Come in, Charlie?"

"Go for Charlie. Over."

"We don't have any records of either man buying a plane ticket, Charlie," Laura said.

"Of course not," Wilson sighed, "That'd be too easy. Thanks, Laura."

He turned to Stewart and said, "No one kills a family and then books a flight to Mexico with their credit card and driver's license."

"Think they both got fakes?"

"Well, it's not like they were hurting for money," Wilson reasoned.

"You're about to miss the turn!" Wilson nearly flew by the farm road that led out to the Aricksons' vineyard. "Why aren't these damn roads marked?" Wilson complained, instantly cutting the steering right, wheels squealing, sending rubble into the air, and creating a dust cloud, "I would have flown right past it if I didn't have you, Magellan."

"Hey, you know, the next exit is just a mile away. I think that's a better alternative than dying, so…" Stewart chimed in.

"Stewart, you've never died with me behind the wheel, and you never will," Wilson said, and then frowned, "I hope."

Stewart graced that answer with a snort.

The Aricksons' home was two miles down the unmarked farm road. You had to get through an enormous wrought-iron entry gate with a six-foot cursive A in its center to get into the place. There was a call box to the left of the drive with a keypad on it.

"Great," Wilson said as they sat outside the entrance. "You need a code to get in. Ready to get some exercise?"

"You mean, climb the gate?"

"No, I was actually thinking of some burpees."

"They say sarcasm is the lowest form of wit... and you're just the lowest form of all."

"That was completely uncalled for!" Wilson said, holding his hand to his heart.

The two made their way over the fifteen-foot gate and walked the quarter-mile up to the Aricksons' home. The place looked like a Tuscan mansion. It was two stories of stucco and stone topped with Spanish tile on a lawn that looked like a paradise landscape. The house had three major wings, each of which had large balconies and front porches. It was a short hike up to an impressive set of marble stairs that led to the towering front door of the house. When the two detectives made it to the door, a frazzled housekeeper was there to answer their knock.

"Seriously," Stewart said, a little out of breath. "Now she decides to show up."

"Hello, my name is Bethany, and I'm the housekeeper here. It's so awful what happened," the well-built woman in her early thirties with cropped blond hair said as she broke into sobs.

Despite everything that was going on, Wilson couldn't help but think that she was the best-looking housekeeper he'd ever seen. Weirdly enough, there was some sophistication even in the way she sobbed. What she was doing as a housekeeper was beyond him.

"Hi, my name is Charles," Wilson said, his voice a little softer than its usual register.

Instantly, Stewart whipped toward him.

"Here," Wilson handed her a tissue, "...now, Bethany, we're going to ask you some questions. Do you mind telling us where you were last night?"

"I was back in the maid's quarters after seven last night," she bawled. "It's about three hundred yards or so from the house, but a decent-sized partition separates me, so I had no idea until I woke up this morning and came in at five a.m. that something was wrong."

"What made you think something was wrong?" Wilson investigated.

"What do you mean?" the maid replied.

"What was it at five in the morning that made you think that something awful had happened?"

"There was no one at the house."

"How would you know that at five in the morning?"

"Because Steve is usually up for a morning swim by then."

"Does he swim at five in the morning every morning?" Stewart asked.

"The majority of the time," she replied. "And even if he doesn't, he comes down to the kitchen to have coffee."

"An early riser, he is," Wilson stated.

"Yes," Bethany said, nodding her head. "But I could tell things were wrong when I started my routine chores."

"Go on," Wilson encouraged.

"I can't explain it, really, but things were somewhat off."

"Did you notice any blood anywhere?"

"There was no blood, but the door wasn't locked, and the alarm wasn't set. I didn't think much about the alarm because Steve would turn it off whenever he got up. However, he never left the door unlocked. And there were things out of place that I knew weren't the way they were the night before."

"Like, like what?"

"Well, for one, the pictures on the mantel were knocked over, and one was missing," she said.

"A missing picture? How do you know there was a picture missing from the mantle?" Wilson asked.

"There are certain spots for the pictures on the mantle with black frame holders. I could easily tell this picture was missing because it was a picture of the whole family," Bethany said.

"Anything else?" Wilson asked.

"I know this is silly, but there were what looked like drag marks on the carpet," the maid answered, not crying so much now that they were talking.

"Drag marks?" Stewart raised an eyebrow. "Like blood?"

"No, I said there was no blood. There were odd marks found like someone had dragged furniture around the house all night or something. And quite a few of the rugs were wadded up. That's just not normal because I straighten everything up and vacuum before I leave for the evening."

"We're going to look around the place," Wilson said. "If you don't mind, just stay put in here while we look."

"Of course."

"What are your thoughts?" Wilson asked as they disappeared down the hall.

"I think maybe she had something going on with Mr. Arickson, but she didn't have anything to do with this," she answered.

"Why do you think something was going on?"

"Sounding a little crushed there, Willy," Stewart said, throwing him a sidelong glance.

"Okay, never, ever call me Willy again, or I'm putting in for a change of partners," Wilson said.

"She calls her boss Steve, not Steven or Mr. Arickson. And he gets up at five to swim or have coffee? If that isn't code for something else, then I don't know what is."

"Hmm."

"What?"

"It seems weird that Arickson would cheat on a supermodel babe with a maid."

"She's not exactly Alice from The Brady Bunch," Stewart said with a chuckle.

"This place is so big, it's intimidating," Wilson said, changing the subject.

There were thirteen bedrooms, three kitchens, a children's wing, and a master wing that opened onto its courtyard with a swimming pool. Wilson hardly knew where to begin.

"I guess we should start with the Arickson's bedroom," he said, looking around.

"Sounds like a plan," Stewart nodded and then took off down a long hallway.

Wilson followed, and they ended up right in the master suite. By the looks of the master bedroom, it was evident that the foul play had started here. A bedside lamp was knocked over, and a bedside table drawer was thrown face down with its contents scattered. Among the papers and reading glasses was a small handgun.

"He must have known what was coming," Wilson said.

"That is her side of the bed," Stewart responded.

"How do you know that?"

"The other side has his reading glasses," she answered, pointing at the black-framed glasses on the nightstand.

"How do you know those are his and not his wife's?" Wilson asked.

"There is a pair of floral reading glasses and a romantic novel on this side of the bed, so unless he was very feminine, I am going to say this was Mrs. Arickson's side."

"Nice. Good observation, Cass."

The two then went through the rest of the house and found little pieces of evidence here and there that proved what the coroner had said. They had been drugged. There were signs of a struggle near the beds in both the master bedroom and the kids' rooms, but then the struggles seemed to stop shortly afterward.

As they were wrapping up, Wilson said, "The killers must have doped them up and dragged them out."

"Why not just kill them in the house and leave them here instead of risking getting busted? That would have saved time and work for the killers."

"It was more personal," Wilson explained. "They didn't just want to shoot the Aricksons and leave them to die. They wanted to make a point."

"That's a good theory," Stewart said as they entered the living room.

"We're going to need to tape this off and have you go somewhere else for a while," Wilson said to Bethany, who'd followed them from a distance. "Are there any other employees who may be stopping in?"

"I've already contacted all of them," Bethany said. "And I arranged to stay with my sister."

"Does she live close by?" Stewart inquired.

"About fifteen minutes away."

"Go ahead and leave us your number and stay close," Stewart said. "We may need you to come in again later for further questioning. I wouldn't recommend taking an out-of-state vacation until this is over."

"Are you telling me I'm not allowed to or shouldn't?"

"Just don't leave town," Stewart said firmly.

"I hadn't planned on it."

"Good."

***

The vans pulled up just as they were heading out — half a dozen decked out with antennae and satellite dishes all over. Stewart barked a curse and froze.

Wilson grumbled, "Here we go."

He could just make out the words over the already-increasing roar of the crowd.

"Is that him?"

"The detective?"

"What's his name?"

"Are we live? Are we live?"

"Call Atlanta."

"That's the guy?"

Stewart looked over at him. She'd gone pale.

"What do we do?"

"Just get to the car," he replied, trying not to move his lips in case the cameras were rolling, "and remember, no comment. Repeat after me."

"No comment," she said.

"Good," Wilson said. "Just keep saying that."

The two cops quickly made their way toward the car. They hadn't gotten halfway there when they were surrounded.

"Detective. Detective! Any truth to the rumors that the Aricksons were found hanging together?"

"No comment."

"Do you have any suspects, Detective? Any leads?"

"No comment."

"Detective, could this have been a murder-suicide?"

"No comment."

"Detective, do you suspect cult involvement?"

"No comment."

"Detective, was this the work of Muslim extremists?"

"Muslim… what…? No comment."

"Detective!"

"Detective!"

"Detective?"

"Detective!"

"DETECTIVE!"

Finally, they were back in the car, and Wilson could breathe again. He felt like he'd just run a marathon. He had never wanted a cigarette so badly, but he knew the Chief would freak out if it appeared on television.

"Jesus," Stewart managed once they were a few blocks away.

Yup! was all Wilson could think of saying. He kept checking the rearview mirror. A couple of enterprising journalists had made it to their vans in time to catch up with him. He debated using his sirens to escape but felt that would only worsen things.

"We gotta find these two guys before this gets any worse," she said.

"That would be ideal, yes," Wilson acknowledged.

"Shit," Stewart murmured.

Something was off about her voice—something that caused a bead of sweat to fall on the back of Wilson's neck. He couldn't quite place it, though. It was probably just the press setting off her nerves. They drove in silence for a while before Wilson finally spoke again.

"You were kind of harsh back there, Cass."

"Was I?"

"A little; it sounded like you were making her a suspect."

"Perhaps I was."

"She didn't have anything to do with this. She's just a maid that Arickson was getting his rocks off with."

"That's exactly why I need to make her a suspect. I don't know where your blood is when it comes to her, but it certainly ain't in your brain. And if that doesn't make her a suspect, I don't know what would."

"We have our suspects already. Don't let yourself stray. We're after Smith and Herring, remember?"

"I'm just trying not to be too narrow-minded in this situation. Sometimes you miss the big red flags right in front of you because you're too focused on something off in the distance."

"Being focused is hardly myopia. We've got our guys. We just need to find them. That means we can't let anything like a grieving mistress throw us off their scent."

"You're right," she admitted.

Wilson knew they needed some kind of break in the case that would lead them to one or both suspects. He knew it might be tough to track them down, but the hardest part was done. They had the suspects, and everything was falling into place to prove precisely what had happened. It would just be a matter of time before something came up that would lead them to the killer. He had a perfect record of catching the bad guy up to this point and had no intention of breaking his fourteen-year streak on such a big case.

"Wilson? Over," the radio crackled, but it was Detective Richard, not Laura.

"Wilson here. Over."

"We may have found the murder weapon while combing the house. You will not believe who has been pulled into the middle of this mess. Get here as soon as possible, man. This just took a turn I've never seen before."

Wilson used the sirens this time. To hell with what the reporters thought.

7

An Unexpected Turn

"I swear I had nothing to do with this, Wilson! You must know that I didn't," shouted Officer Cooper.

Charles stepped back as the Chief hauled Officer Cooper away in handcuffs. Cooper's eyes bulged under his dark-filled eyes, and his face was so red that it blended with the color of his hair. Wilson couldn't process the scene he had just walked into.

"What the hell is this?" Wilson asked as he watched the Chief take off with the newbie in the backseat.

"We believe we found the knife used for the murders," Richard told him.

"So, why are they dragging Cooper away?"

"The knife came from his family's deli."

"What? How would they even know that?"

"The dumb shit used a knife with the deli logo carved into the handle. Can you believe that?"

"Where was it discovered?"

"In a drawer that was slightly open with many other knives inside. Only a cop knows not to hide stuff out in the open like that. We're lucky we found it. The thing would have blended in with the other knives if it hadn't been for the handle."

"Was there blood on it?"

"There was no blood, and it looked like it had been washed with bleach. The officers are taking it to the lab to run a few tests and see what they can get from it."

"What about Herring and Smith?" Wilson asked.

"That is what makes this so complicated. We need to figure out what is going on there — what the connection might be among the three of them."

"Yes, we do," Wilson said, concurring. "I'm going to head over to the office to try to sort some of this out. Call me if anything new comes up."

"The way it's going now, something will come. I just hope it doesn't get any more screwed up than it already is," Richard said.

Wilson left Detective Stewart at the crime scene and headed for the station. Finding the murder weapon usually clears things up in a case, but in that instant, it had just muddied the waters in a big way. There were no apparent ties between the two suspects and Officer Cooper. There was also no motive that Wilson could see right away for Cooper to get involved. Wilson saw him as a no-name kid who had worked slinging cold cuts for years and joined the force, so he could feel like his life meant something. Nothing pointed toward him being the kind of guy who would hack up a family. Wilson recalled how squeamish he had been about even looking at the faces of the victims. He wondered if it was all just an act.

Perhaps Cooper was some kind of demented mastermind.

The more Wilson thought about it, the less likely it seemed that the rookie detective could have had a hand in the murder. He had worked in homicide long enough to compile a list of psychopaths' traits, and Cooper had none. Wilson had been face-to-face with many unlikely murderers, so he knew that they came in all packages, but Cooper didn't match any of the characteristics of someone capable of committing a crime as heinous as the Arickson murders. How did a knife from his family's deli get into that house if he didn't do it?

He spotted the news vans clustered around the front of the building and decided to snake around the long way and get in through the back. He knew that the Chief would make him pay for the chaos he had caused at some point.

It didn't do him nearly as much good as he'd hoped. Marquez was seated on a bench near the door as if she were waiting for him. Before she could even say a word, Wilson held up his hand and shook his head.

"Uh-uh, no way I'm saying anything right now."

"C'mon, Detective," Marquez protested, "somebody's going to have to say something eventually — especially now that you're looking at one of your own as the suspect."

He almost stopped to demand to know where she'd heard it. Almost. It was one last second of sanity that stopped him. He knew there was no getting out of it if he went down that rabbit hole right then.

He turned, glared, and said, "No comment."

She nodded and made a note, "So, you and Stewart are running the investigation?"

"I'm the lead detective; why?"

Marquez shrugged, "No reason. I went to school with Stewart."

"That's special," he said. "Well, why don't you go bother Stewart then? I mean, if you're insisting on bothering someone. I'd rather you go back to covering pie-eating contests or whatever the hell you used to do."

Marquez chuckled, "Oh, she'd never talk to me. Back in the day, we had a small issue with a guy. Not a good loser, your partner."

"This is fascinating stuff, Marquez," Wilson said.

He couldn't help wondering which guy would pick the reporter over Stewart, and he thought Marquez was attractive enough but nowhere near Stewart's league.

"You sleep with her?" Marquez asked.

Wilson was taken aback by the question, "Jesus Christ! There's no way that falls under the public's right to know."

Marquez shrugged, "I'm just saying, watch yourself. That one's trouble."

He'd had enough of this, "Just go crawl back under your rock, Marquez."

Before she could reply, he threw open the door and stormed inside. As he walked through the station, he started to collect himself. He knew there was no point in losing his cool. There was too much going on; there were too many eyes on him now. If he started acting wild, people would talk, and he sure didn't need that.

"Hey, boss," said Ashley, a young woman from the tech department, as she pulled a chair up to Wilson's desk to face the detective.

Wilson was deep in thought, but he snapped to attention when she spoke.

"Hey there. Have you found anything out for me on our suspects yet?"

"Yes, I have."

"Right now, I could use it."

"So, we went digging in all of Declan Herring's hard drives and computer files, and we didn't find anything that hinted at him purchasing a plane ticket."

"That was not what I wanted to hear," Wilson mumbled.

"We did find some text messages and emails Herring had sent to a colleague of his. It looks like Mr. Herring was reaching out to this guy. Several texts and emails discuss how Herring felt like someone had been following him."

"Really?" Wilson sat up in his chair. "Did they say why he thought someone would be after him?"

"They didn't, but it was clear that Herring felt threatened by something or, more specifically, someone. And when we investigated Smith's phone records and followed up with his wife, we found the same thing. He had a suspicion that someone was stalking him."

"So, our two suspects felt they were being watched before the murders, then?" Wilson asked, agitated that the information brought more questions than answers.

"That's how it appears. Here are the exchanges if you want to go over them," Ashley said as she dropped a stack of papers on Wilson's already-cluttered desk.

Wilson thanked Ashley and started sifting through the emails and texts. He noticed that both men began to send out distressing messages around the same time, about a month before the murders. He already knew that Smith had been acting strangely after the conversation with his wife, and he couldn't figure out why neither of these men had come forward if they were so worried.

The messages got increasingly urgent as time passed. The last week of messages from Michael Smith looked like the rantings of a paranoid schizophrenic. Both men sent messages to only one friend and no one else. Michael sent them to a former colleague who had worked on the Fireburner project with him but had since moved to Seattle to teach engineering at the University of Washington. On the other hand, Herring was in contact with a friend in the area — a man whom Wilson found out through a little more research was an old college friend. Smith and Herring never contacted one another unless they had cell phones purchased under an alias they used to communicate with. If that was the case, Wilson knew he might never track down the phones that would link the two men. His best bet was to track down the men themselves.

Stewart walked into his office at the precinct that afternoon. She had an air of sadness about her that made it difficult for him to concentrate on reading his messages. He was still hell-bent on finding the suspects, but one look at her face, and he had to say something.

"Something bothering you, Cass?" Charles asked.

She sighed and took a seat beside him. "Your office is a mess," she said, looking around the small office with its scattered paperwork.

He suddenly felt the need to explain himself. "With the case going on, I have not had time to…." Then, upon realizing it, he shook his head. "Hey, don't change the subject on me. What's bothering you?"

She sighed. "It's Cooper. How could they even *think* he had something to do with those gruesome murders? I've known him most of my life. The dude can hardly hurt a fly. He is so harmless; I sometimes wonder why he joined the force in the first place," she said.

The sadness in her voice was glaring now.

Fighting back the urge to hold her and whisper comforting words into her ears, he opted to say instead, "Cooper has always been a nice guy. I don't believe he did it either, but we can do nothing about it, Cass. I'm sorry."

"Yes, there is."

He blinked, "And what would that be?"

She wiped a tear off the bottom of her left eye. Her expression was suddenly set and determined as she said, "We can find the goddamn bastard who did this and throw his ass in jail."

This time it was his turn to sigh, "I'm trying my best. You know that, right?"

"Yes, I do. So am I. But this isn't a case of our superiors breathing down our necks anymore. An innocent friend is in custody for something he didn't do. We *have* to find the killer."

Charles was unsure how Cooper would react if he heard her say those words, and it would surely stir up mixed feelings in the rookie cop. On the one hand, the woman he had so obviously been crushing on cared about him enough to shed a tear, but she referred to him as a "friend."

Charles said, "I'll find them."

"We will find them," she corrected. "This is my case as much as yours. It's personal for me."

He nodded as their eyes met. For some reason, Charles could not bring himself to look away. He could tell she had been crying, and he resisted the urge to wipe a tear off her soft cheek.

He coughed before saying, "I love that we are fired up and all, but it still doesn't change the fact that we have no real, concrete lead."

"Yes, we do," she said. "We have our suspects."

"Suspects who we can't seem to find anywhere in the city. They could be halfway across the world as we speak."

"They have close friends and family. Someone among them would have to know where they'd go if they were ever on the run."

"Well, we can't question everyone close to Michael and Herring until we are certain they did it."

"No, we can't. Not unless we are certain they did it," she said, biting a long, pink fingernail.

Charles nodded and asked, "Do you have any ideas? We need to get moving with *something,* or the Chief will have our asses."

"I just might have something in mind, but it seems like too much of a long shot."

"I don't care how long a shot it is. I'll take it as long as it's coming from you."

Stewart glanced at him. He could tell she was surprised by his confidence in her.

She said, "The killer drugged the victims with heroin. Where do you think he would have gotten his hands on it?"

Charles frowned, "Not from any pharmacist's counter."

"Exactly. He must have scored the dope from the dealer. If we can somehow get the dealer to admit he sold drugs to either of them, we have them."

He chuckled, "Well, you certainly weren't kidding about it being a long shot. He could have used any of the city's dozens of dealers. And then there's the next-to-impossible chance of getting a drug dealer to snitch on his customers."

"From what I gathered about the suspects, they wouldn't be comfortable carrying a bag of heroin from one end of the city to another. It has to be somewhere close to their home."

"Whose home? Herring's or Michael's?"

"I'll need a list of all the possible dealers within a one-kilometer radius of their places. With any luck, the closest one to either of them would be our dealer."

He nodded, "That seems fair enough. Give me a minute."

He walked out of the office to the records department, where he obtained the information they needed — a list of suspected heroin drug dealers and their possible locations. When he returned to his office, Stewart had already spread out a city map over his desk. There were two blue pins stuck on the map, denoting Michael and Herring's residences.

"Let's see which of these scoundrels operates closest to our guys, now shall we," he said, pulling out half a dozen red pins from his desk drawer.

They spent the next ten minutes sticking these red pins on various locations on the map, and they looked at the results with frowns on their faces in the end.

"We have three possible candidates here," she said. "Two next to Michael. And one next to Herring."

"My money is on Michael," he said.

"I don't know. This dealer stays close to Herring. He could be our guy."

"Look at it this way. All three of them have suspected fake establishments, which they use as covers. A two-star restaurant, a wacky bakery, and a decent club. Where do you think our boys will be most comfortable going? I don't know about you, but my money is on the club."

She smiled, "You are smart, Charles. This has to be our dealer."

"Even if he is? How do we get him to come with us for questioning? Even if we raid the place, there's a chance he could go underground."

She gave him a lopsided smile, "When was the last time you went undercover, Charles?"

***

The club was the loudest Charles had ever been in. Thankfully, it wasn't the weekend, so the building wasn't overcrowded with clubbers. He and Stewart had enough space to pass through and find a good seat in a corner. They were dressed very casually. He wore a white shirt that exposed the muscles in his arms and tight blue jeans. She wore a black dress that rode as high as the upper part of her thighs, exposing her long legs. The dress also exposed enough cleavage to cause any man who passed them to suck in their breath. The club area was dark, with disco lights flashing all around, offering the only illumination source.

"So, what's next?" she asked, raising her voice so he could hear her over the sound of the blaring music. "Do we tell the waitress we want something special when she comes to take our order?"

"Hell no! That's what a cop would do," he said. "We have to look like we're having fun. Down a few drinks, get drunk a bit, and observe everything here. When we finally make our move, it will seem like we just want to take the fun up a notch."

"All right," she said.

The waitress came a few minutes later, and they ordered bottles of champagne. Once they were done with the bottles, more drinks came flying in. Charles wasn't much of a drinker, but he could hold his liquor well enough. He maintained his focus and did his best to observe what was happening around him.

"You see that guy at four o'clock?" he asked.

"The one in the blue suit?"

"Yes."

"What about him?"

"Notice how he goes about meeting various clubbers with a smile on his face as if they were old friends. He had passed some tables a few minutes ago, and he didn't give them a second glance."

"You think that's our dealer?" she asked.

"I'm fairly certain he is. They wouldn't let any of the waitresses touch that shit."

"Do we make the order now?"

"Not yet. We still have to make anyone watching believe we are regular clubgoers."

She smiled seductively, "Good, because I'm in the mood to dance."

Before he could say anything, she dragged him toward the dance floor. For the sake of not blowing their cover, he followed her. Charles could not remember the last time he tapped his feet to the rhythm of a song, much less danced. The idea of "letting his hair down" felt alien to him. Nevertheless, he did his best to play along as best he could. She, however, was something different. Stewart moved her body like a snake. There were instances where he struggled to control his excitement as she pushed her body against his. They spent the next ten minutes gyrating on the floor to the beat of the music.

There and then, Charles felt something. There was a form of electricity between them. It was so strong that they struggled to catch their breath. Her lips, slightly parted and only inches from his, seemed to beckon to him, begging him to take them with his mouth.

"Are you okay?" she asked.

"Yeah. Must be all the weed in the air."

She looked at him strangely, "Yeah. I guess you're not used to the club environment. I think we look convincing enough. Let's get back to our table and make our move."

He agreed. They walked hand in hand to their corner. He waited for a few more minutes before signaling the waitress.

When she arrived, he said casually, “The lady and I were wondering if we could get something else — something off the menu?”

The waitress smiled and said, “I’ll be with you in a bit.” Then she walked away.

Charles watched her disappear into a back room.

He said, “Now she’ll talk to the dealer. He will confirm with some bouncers if it’s safe to approach us. Hopefully, they will tell him it is after watching us all night.”

A few minutes later, the man in the blue suit appeared out of nowhere. He had that same smile as he scanned the room for his “old friends.”

“He’s here,” Charles said. “Let’s not stare.”

The man walked casually toward a table a few feet away from them. Charles fought the urge to stare at him as he talked with a couple. He soon finished with them and came to stand beside them.

“Guys! You didn’t tell me you were coming around today,” he said, looking genuinely happy to see them. “The waitress told me you two were around. I’d have missed you otherwise.”

Charles feigned confusion, then slowly let his expression shift into sudden realization.

He coughed, “Yes, we didn’t want to disturb you. It’s good to see you, though. Have a seat.”

The man took a seat beside Stewart, grinning from ear to ear. Charles was impressed by her performance as the stereotypical *dumb bikini model.*

“So,” the man in the blue suit said. “What can I get you?”

Charles acted like he was reluctant to speak.

The man said, “Don’t worry, buddy. No one will hear you over this music. By the way, you can call me Dash.”

“Okay, Dash. I need enough heroin to last the lady and me for the night.”

Dash nodded. He told them his price. Charles agreed to pay, and the man handed Stewart a brown envelope. Charles, in turn, handed him some money.

“Nice doing business with you, bud,” Dash said with a wide grin as he made to leave their table.

“Hold on a bit,” Charles said. The man paused, raising an eyebrow. Charles continued to talk, “I’m having a party in two days. I’ll need a much larger amount of product to add some kick to my party.”

Dash looked from him to Stewart. He was weighing his options. Charles hoped the chance to make a lot of money would far outweigh his need to stay cautious if he suspected anything.

"We'll need to talk in my office. Do you want to come now or later?"

Charles looked at Stewart, "Well, I guess we have a couple of minutes to spare before heading out. Let's go."

"Follow me," Dash said.

He took them into the back room, up a flight of stairs, and into a small office. The only visible furniture was a table and chairs on either side, and the wood looked older than the entire club. Looking at the shabby-looking place, Charles was confident his suspicions were correct. Dash was small-time. Slinging dope in the club with the owner's permission just to make ends meet. He most likely had a sizable percentage of his sales going to the club owner and was eager to secure a big deal he could deliver outside the club. That would mean he could keep the profits for himself.

"So, how much product do you want?"

"It's my baby's birthday; about fifty people are attending, so… you do the math," Charles said, smiling at Stewart, seated beside him.

Dash licked his lips, "You want enough… Harry, to cover fifty people?"

"Not just Harry. Coke and acid too."

"It's gonna cost you."

Charles smiled, “I should think so, seeing that it has already cost you so much.”

“What do you mean?” Dash said, with a confused look on his face.

“I mean that my beautiful companion here has been recording this conversation since we got here.”

Stewart perked up and waved, pulling out a small recording device she had hidden in her bosom. Dash nearly jumped out of his seat in shock.

“Don’t bother reaching for a gun. Things can only deteriorate for you. That recorder is transmitting live to our team outside. We couldn’t come into the club with guns, but you’ll be in trouble if anything happens to us.”

Charles stared intently at Dash, seeing the cogs behind the frightened eyes turning. Fortunately, he concluded that the cops were right. The fight went out of him instantly, and he slumped back to his seat like a defeated lion.

“What do you want? To arrest me?”

“If we wanted to arrest, trust me, we wouldn’t need to go through all this trouble,” Stewart said.

Charles said, “We didn’t come here to arrest you, Dash. At least not now. We came here for information on someone you may have sold heroin to a while back.”

"Rules of the game, gentlemen," Dash said in a mock-hurt voice. "I would love to snitch on my clients, but that's a big no-no around these parts."

"Well, what if I tell you that your customer snitched on you? He drugged a family of five using your product, kidnapped them, and butchered them to death."

Charles noticed a change coming over the dealer. No doubt, he had heard about the Aricksons. Now he knew how big of a mess he was in.

Choosing his moment, Charles decided to drive the point home by saying, "We have your product. If we run a test on it and its quality matches the one used by the murderer, you could be brought in as an accomplice."

"Enough, okay. I'll help you, but only because I don't approve of my product being used for something as messed up as that," Dash said, clinging to a loophole in his code of conduct as a peddler.

Stewart did not waste a second. She took out two photographs from her purse and handed them to Dash one at a time. The first was Herring. Dash shook his head.

Charles studied him and instinctively knew he wasn't lying. "I've never seen this dude in my life."

The second was a picture of Michael. Charles held his breath as Dash squinted at the picture, and he suddenly cursed.

“You know him?” Charles asked.

“Yeah... this fella came into the club three nights ago and placed a special order just like you two did — a fancy-dressed guy who seemed better off playing golf in some country club. I usually avoid selling to such people, but he sold me some bullshit story about his woman needing a fix. So, I hooked him up. I knew his ass was trouble.”

Charles wanted to mention that the dealer’s love for money would always cloud his better judgment, but he decided against it. He wasn’t in the habit of handing out sincere criticism to potentially dangerous men. After all, he was on the side that wanted them behind bars… not prosperous!

“We are going to leave now. If anything happens between now and when we get to our team, you will have to answer to the entire police department. We won’t press charges against you for dealing, but you can be sure we will be back. So, I suggest you find yourself a legit means of living. Think of this as a second chance.”

When Charles and Stewart were safely in his car, driving back to the precinct, they burst into laughter.

“I can’t believe he fell for that. If he didn’t, though, we would be dead.”

Charles said, “He had to. There was no way you could tell we were doing this off the record.”

"Do you think the Chief would approve?" Stewart said.

"I think he would care more about the results. Now we know who the killer is. We know who to look for, even though we can't use this recording in court."

Stewart nodded, "And now we can get poor Cooper out of jail."

She looked at Charles and smiled. "We make a pretty good team, don't we?"

"Yes," he replied. "We certainly do."

Wilson's head was spinning between the messages he had and the discovery of the murder weapon. The case had seemed clear-cut enough when the fingerprints came back, but it was getting more tangled by the second. Who was threatening both men? And was the person aware of a plan to kill Steven Arickson?

Wilson decided to question Cooper in custody with so much to figure out. He was about to head down to the county jail to meet Cooper when he got a phone call from the Chief on his way down.

"Cooper has been cleared," the Chief told him.

"What?" he asked.

"He's been cleared. We will keep him on paid leave while the investigation is pending, but we've released him to go home."

"So, does that mean the knife *wasn't* his?"

"No, it was from his family's deli, but Cooper didn't hack those people up."

Wilson felt as if the ground was being pulled from underneath him. He was used to fitting pieces of a puzzle together, but it started to feel like someone was handing him pieces that went into another puzzle. The further he got into the case, the less sense it made.

The Chief explained that the spotlight had been taken off of Cooper because he had an airtight alibi. No one knew it when they were hauling him off in handcuffs, but Cooper had been with another senior detective, Detective Morris, all that evening until his shift with Richard started. He was trying to get extra training to help him move up the ranks faster. When Morris caught wind that Cooper had been booked as a suspect, he rushed to Cooper's defense and got him off the hook. While that did manage to take the target off Cooper's back, it did not explain how the knife made it to the crime scene.

"You know where Cooper went?" Wilson asked.

"I assume home."

"Thanks, Chief. See you later at the station."

"Hang on," the Chief said. "What's this? I heard about you talking to the reporter. That broad?"

His voice was calm, but a knife edge was tucked somewhere. Wilson could tell.

"More like she's talking to me," Wilson explained. "All I've given her are *no comments*."

"And the army of parasites parked outside my office window? Did you talk to them?"

"I've managed to avoid them so far. They won't get anything from me, boss."

"And your guys? This is important, hear me?!?"

"I hear. My guys are solid. They're not going to start spilling."

"These aren't your average mooks, Wilson," the Chief said. "We've got big guns out there. The mayor hasn't stopped calling me since all this started. Swear to God that the guy's heart will blow right out of his chest. It would be best if you kept your eyes on your guys. I swear to Christ, any leaks, I will have your balls in a jar on my desk."

Wilson reassured him, "I understand."

"Find your guy, Detective," the Chief said lowly. "Find him, or we'll all be out of a job."

The Chief hung up before Wilson could reply. He stared down at his phone before making a call to Laura to ask where Officer Cooper lived.

"Hasn't he been through enough today?" Laura asked.

"Something weird is going on here, and I need to talk to him if I want to start making sense of this."

"Did the Chief OK this?"

"I didn't ask," Wilson admitted.

Laura was hesitant about giving Wilson the information, but she knew him well and trusted his hunches. She had no idea what he had up his sleeve but knew that he had an impressive track record, and he seemed sure about whatever he planned to do next. She rattled off the address; it was an apartment in a low-rent area. Wilson pulled over and switched routes. He was going to visit Cooper. He may have had an alibi, but he still had some explaining to do.

8

Endless Possibilities

Cooper's apartment was right above the family deli he'd worked at. It was on a run-down street lined with cars held together with hangers and duct tape. There were no expensive coffee shops or high-end boutiques like on Wilson's side of town. It looked like they had another month in them at best.

Cooper had a unique way of living, that was for sure. Wilson felt a hard ball of pity form in his stomach for the rookie cop who had just been dragged off a scene and turned into a suspect. Pity was not something Wilson often let himself feel.

"Cooper, are you there?" he called from outside the apartment door.

The building smelled like stale cigarettes and melted wax from cheap convenience-store candles.

"I just want to talk. I know it's been a rough day."

Cooper answered the door with a hangdog expression on his face. He didn't say a word at first; he just shuffled to the side of the threshold to let Wilson cross. Cooper let out a low, rumbling sob when they finally sat on his ratty futon, his only living room furniture.

"I did not cause any harm to that family."

"How did the knife get there, Cooper?"

"I have no idea. I don't."

"Does anyone else work in the shop?"

"My mom and pop are there, but that is it. And there's no way they hacked up a family and hung them like that. Please, don't put them in…."

"We aren't going to put them in holding," Wilson assured him. "But we may need to ask them some questions. The fact is, Cooper, that knife came from your family's deli beneath us. That means the killer was in there at some point."

"But don't we already know who the murderers are?"

"I thought we did, but this is getting increasingly messed up with every piece of evidence we get."

Wilson and Cooper sat in his depressing apartment and talked for another half hour. The two talked about work and what brought Cooper to the force in the first place. Wilson was surprised when he found out that Cooper had joined the homicide department to impress a girl. Wilson didn't have any more questions for the rookie, but he could see that he was in the wrong place and could use some company.

Talking about Cassidy, Wilson said with a chuckle, "That's a serious crush. But she is something. I'll give you that."

Cooper replied hesitantly, "I see the thing going on between you two. I know I don't have a chance against a guy like you. Plus, I respect you. I was trying hard to get her, but I'm going to step back on the whole Cassidy thing. She was probably just hanging out with me when she did that out of pity for me."

Wilson thought about Cooper's statement. He felt for the guy. It was painfully clear that a girl like Cassidy would never give Cooper the time of day, even if he had given up making sliced turkey sandwiches to work on homicides.

"You're lucky, you know," Cooper said.

"Am I?"

"Yeah, you are. You have it all. You're good-looking, and you're the top dog at work. Wilson, you could easily get any girl you wanted. Things aren't that easy for the rest of us."

Charles Wilson thought about the rookie officer's words. He found it amusing that someone saw him as lucky.

Wilson was in his thirties and had never had a meaningful relationship with a woman. He may have been the best at what he did. Wilson had no one to share it with — no friends to have a beer with when there was a big break in a case, no girlfriend to celebrate big promotions with, and no parents to call when he was honored with some award or recognition. He didn't even have a pet because he was too busy with work. Being lucky was the last thing Wilson ever considered for himself. Successful, maybe, but never lucky.

"You've got more than you realize, Cooper," he finally said.

"Like what?"

"Do you have any friends? Any buddies you shoot the shit with?"

"Just a few."

"What about your family? I know your mom and dad are nearby."

"We're all pretty close. I have two brothers. They live in town, and we get together on occasion. They've got more going on than me, but they make time to have a beer once a week."

"All I have is work, Cooper. That's all. And right now, I have a case that is wrecking my brain like nothing ever has, so I better get going," he said as he lifted off the futon and offered Cooper his hand. "You take care. I'll solve this case, and you'll be back to work. And if you or your parents can think of anything, call us."

As Wilson left the house, he felt confident that Cooper hadn't played any role in the murder of the Aricksons. The kid was too soft to have done something like that and had no motive whatsoever. Still, the mystery of the deli knife plagued Wilson. He doubted that either Smith or Herring happened to snag a knife from the deli one day or found the thing lying around.

Whoever did the slashing must have left the knife there on purpose.

Wilson wondered if the two suspects had a third accomplice yet to be discovered. If that was the case, he had more work to do. They had prints that pointed them to Herring and Smith and a motive. The third mystery murderer hadn't left anything behind other than a knife that belonged to a rookie cop's family deli. That hardly made things any easier for Wilson. He'd be at a dead end if no DNA or prints came back on the blade. The third murderer could have been anyone Herring and Smith hired to help them pull the thing off. The only clue he had so far was that they happened to be at the Coopers' deli at some point to get the knife.

***

The following day, Wilson got a phone call from the lab. The knife did have fingerprints… Michael Smith's. That all but eliminates the third suspect. Wilson was happy to hear the news. Still, he wanted to know how the murderer ended up with the knife. He headed back to the deli with a picture of Smith to talk to Cooper's parents.

When he arrived, the place was under siege. News vans lined the streets. To get away from it all, the Coopers closed the shop. They were still inside, though, looking tired, like they'd aged ten years since he'd last seen them.

He tapped on the glass, ignoring the reporters who tried to swarm him. Mr. Cooper peered out. It took a moment for the man to recognize Wilson. He unlocked the door cautiously and let the Detective inside.

He chatted with the elderly couple and showed them the suspect's picture. Neither of them recognized the face. They would have remembered if they had seen him. Michael's left cheek had been severely burned in a childhood accident. The left side of his face was rippled and polished over with scar tissue. He was not a man someone would forget.

Wilson showed a picture of Declan Herring as well. He had no distinguishing scars or birthmarks, but Wilson hoped the couple would recognize the face. As far as he could tell, the deli didn't get a lot of business, so he thought they would be able to recall their few customers. They stared at Declan's picture with blank expressions and shook their heads in unison. Wilson's interview with the Coopers was a dead end.

"If you can think of any suspicious customers who came in, please give me a call," Wilson said, handing them a card. "I mean anyone and everyone at all."

"We sure will, but we haven't had too many customers lately. Jason and his detective friends are about the only ones we see anymore."

Wilson had nearly forgotten that Jason was Cooper's first name.

"Well, if you think of something, let me know."

"At first, I thought all of these reporters would be good for business," Mrs. Cooper grumbled. "But all they do is make a mess and pry with their questions. Isn't there anything you can do, Detective?"

Wilson shook his head, "Believe me, ma'am; I wish there was."

As Wilson drove back to the precinct, he replayed the seemingly useless conversation he'd just had in the back of his mind. He was salty enough to know that sometimes little, insignificant clues break cases wide open. He thought about everything the Coopers had told him and then thought about the knife.

One statement, in particular, stuck in Wilson's craw: "Jason and his detective friends are about the only people who come in anymore."

The knife showed up at the scene as if by magic, which murder weapons rarely do. Cooper had an alibi that took him away from the scene, but what about the other cops? The ones who popped in and out of the deli with Cooper, who would have access to one of the knives with the family's logo on it?

"Laura, I want you to check on every officer who worked the Arickson scene."

"Will do, Charlie. Can I ask why?"

"I can't say yet, but I want to know where every officer and detective who stepped foot on that scene was from five in the evening until I showed up that night."

9

A Rude Awakening

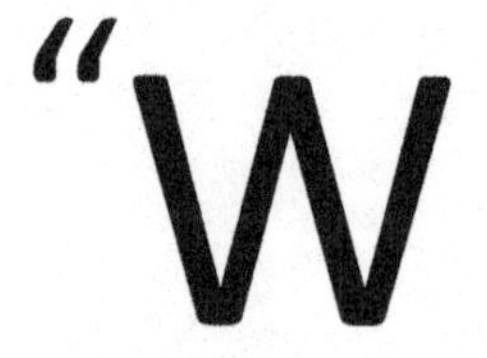

here the hell are you, Wilson?” It was the Chief. Somewhere nearby, a phone was blaring, making it hard to focus.

“I’m just out doing some interviews for the Arickson case,” Wilson answered.

“Are you alone?” he asked.

Charles could hear something strange in the Chief’s voice. It was urgency, or it was fear. He couldn’t pinpoint it, but he was damn sure he’d never heard that tone from the Chief before.

“Yeah, I am. Everything alright, Chief?” Wilson asked, frowning.

“You need to get here now! And don’t tell anyone where you’re going. I mean it. You don’t answer dispatch, your cell phone, or even wave hello to anyone. You get here right now and come straight to my office.”

Wilson paused for a second, a single question going around in his brain. Could he trust the Chief?

“What the hell is going on?” Wilson asked, his voice instinctively mimicking the urgency in the Chief’s voice.

“I will tell you when you get here.”

The line went dead, but Wilson didn’t move. His mind was racing at a thousand miles an hour. He eventually concluded that the Chief could be trusted.

Barely a minute had passed when his phone rang again. This time, it was Cassidy. She probably wanted an update on the case. He nearly answered it out of habit but stopped himself. Before the call even hit his voicemail, Laura was coming through on the radio.

"Charlie, you there? Over."

Charles remained silent.

"Charlie? Charles, pick up. Over."

If she called his cell phone next, she had something big for him. He held his breath as he waited for his phone to stop ringing. His nerves were set on edge just below his skin, and his veins throbbed against his temples. He felt like a predator in pursuit of its prey; his senses were sharp. The only problem was that he had been ordered not to pounce.

From the passenger seat, his phone screeched at him. He didn't need to look to see who it was. He knew it was from Laura. She had a hit. Wilson's best guess was that she knew something about one of the officers on the scene—information that might put him hot on the killer's trail. He wanted nothing more than to answer the call, but he trusted the Chief and was under strict orders.

But the Chief doesn't know what I do, Wilson thought as he grappled with the urge to answer Laura's call. He needed to talk to Laura. He needed to find out whatever it was she found.

Wilson grabbed his phone and held it above the steering wheel, staring at it as he drove. He clenched it in one fist the way you might grasp the neck of a rattlesnake. With his bottom teeth grounded against his top teeth, his fingers curled tighter against the phone's edges as he fought to let the call go. It seemed to ring for eternity. Finally, just before Wilson could click accept on his phone, the call went to voicemail.

She'll leave a message, he thought. *I'll listen to it to see what she has.*

"Charlie, where the hell are you? Over." It was Laura on the radio again.

She hadn't left a message. She probably wanted to tell him personally. The only reason Laura wouldn't leave a message could be that the information was too sensitive. She didn't trust herself to leave whatever she had stumbled on in a message.

"Come on, damn it. Pick up," she said. "Over."

I can't, Wilson thought as he eyed the police radio. *I want to, but I can't.* Again, his phone started up. He slammed his finger into the power button. He'd already made the call — the Chief above Laura.

Wilson drove like a madman the rest of the way to the precinct. He weaved in and out of traffic, nearly taking off the mirrors of a couple of parked cars as he went. He whipped around a family sedan and then nearly plowed into the back of a city garbage truck that had suddenly stopped.

Wilson felt his pulse shoot higher and higher as he slammed his foot from the gas pedal to the brake pedal. His jaw ached from how tightly he clenched his teeth.

When he got to the precinct, he didn't waste time looking for a place to park; he slammed his cruiser into the lieutenant's parking space, got out of the car, and quickly walked toward the precinct door. Just as he was about to enter, he heard a voice he knew belonged to Detective Stewart. She had just pulled in as well. When she saw Wilson, she started calling out for him.

"Wilson! Wait up!" she shouted across the parking lot. "Charles!"

Charles ignored her. He just kept going, his eyes focused on the giant glass doors before him. He heard her footsteps quicken behind him. He also picked up his pace so she wouldn't catch up to him. He'd lost Stewart, but once he got inside, he felt like he was in a nightmare — the kind where you are desperate to get somewhere, but you just can't make it.

It seemed like everyone in the office needed to talk to him. Every time he heard someone start to say his name, his neck muscles throbbed. He didn't make eye contact with anyone as he bounded down the precinct halls, fearing they'd stop him. It was like maneuvering through landmines. He ducked away as soon as his colleagues tried to approach him. He had to get to the Chief. Wilson needed to find out what was happening and get back to Laura to see what she had.

"I'm here," Wilson announced as he opened the Chief's door and closed it.

"Lock it," the Chief ordered.

"What on earth is going on, Chief?"

"Has anyone tried to contact you?"

"Yes, it seems that everyone I've walked by has something they need to tell me."

"Did you speak with any of them?"

Wilson replied, "You told me not to."

"So, you haven't spoken to anyone?"

"Not at all. What is going on? Why am I suddenly on some gag order with the rest of the precinct?"

"We've got one of the suspects," the Chief said, his eyes locked on Wilson's.

"What? Who is it?"

"Michael Smith has surfaced."

"Wait, Smith!?" Wilson gasped. "Where is he?" he asked as he shot up from his chair and grabbed for the doorknob.

"Sit down!" the Chief boomed. "He isn't here."

"Why the hell not?" Wilson demanded.

"Because he is in the hospital. He's being treated at Saint Joseph's."

"The hospital?"

"Yes," the Chief stated emphatically. "He's being treated for several wounds and severe dehydration."

"Wait a minute," Wilson stammered. "What?"

"Smith was found right off of Highway Nineteen."

"The highway that runs out by the old house where the murders took place?" Wilson mumbled as he tried to piece together what all this could mean.

"That's correct. I talked to the husband and wife. They say Smith was half dead and as pale as a ghost when they picked him up. He flagged down a family traveling through the area, and they brought him to the hospital. They said they never do that, but something told them that this guy needed serious help, so they took him to the closest hospital."

"They're lucky he didn't butcher them," Wilson mumbled.

"I've got two officers up at the hospital now guarding him," the Chief said. "They're making sure no one can get to him."

"Guarding *him*? What the hell do we need to protect him from? That man is a monster, Chief. You saw what he did to that family. The world needs to be protected from him, not the other way around."

"Sit down, Wilson," the Chief ordered.

Wilson had remained standing with his hand on the doorknob since he heard that Smith had been caught.

"I need to get to that hospital. I want to talk to that evil piece of…."

"Smith claims he was set up," the Chief said, interrupting Wilson before he could finish his thought.

"I have had a few murderers who have claimed they were set up. They're all set up, Chief," Wilson replied sarcastically. "Don't you know? Nobody in Shawshank is guilty of shit!"

"But do those murderers have wounds that doctors can say were caused by someone else?"

"All that means is that he struggled with the Aricksons when he killed them. I would be shocked if there weren't any wounds. This guy is our crook. He left his fingerprints everywhere."

"There was no struggle before the murder, Wilson. The coroner's report showed that the family was drugged."

"Arickson and his wife were strangled first, though."

"There was no DNA left under their fingernails or on their person. There would be DNA left behind from the kind of wounds Smith has."

"Why don't we just quit skirting around this and tell me what you think is going on, Chief? Because right now, I have no idea what's running through your skull."

"I think that Smith might be telling the truth."

It felt like Wilson's brain lagged. He stood rooted to his spot for a moment, mulling over the Chief's words and all the case evidence in his mind. He finally concluded that he was letting his emotions get the best of him, which was no way for a cop to behave. He decided to approach this matter with a clear mind.

"And that is why he felt like he was being followed," Wilson said as he collapsed back into a chair.

He had been so sure that Smith was at the crime scene that he couldn't see the bigger picture. He had turned Smith into a monster, and there was no going back. But what if he wasn't a monster? What if he was as much of a victim as the Aricksons? Why could he not see it before?

"That is why he was acting so strangely — and the break-in. It all makes sense… but who…."

"That is what we need to find out about next."

"There wasn't a third party or even a second," Wilson said in a low mumble. "It was one person framing two others. I knew someone else was there, but I didn't even consider that Smith wasn't."

"That doesn't mean someone else was there," the Chief replied. "It may have been Herring who framed him. He would have known that Smith had enough ties to Arickson to put it on him. He just messed up and left his prints at the scene."

"It was a cop," Wilson yelled out.

The Chief fixed his gaze on Wilson. He pursed his lips together and took a deep breath through his flared nostrils. Wilson studied the Chief, trying to read him and figure out what he would do with the information Wilson had just vomited out.

He's going to think I'm crazy, Wilson thought. *Or worse.*

"Who else have you told your theory to?" the Chief asked in a low, deliberate voice.

"No one."

"Keep it like that," the Chief advised.

"I know how it sounds, Chief, but…."

"Stop, Wilson," the Chief said. "Look, I realize it may be one of our own."

"You do?" Wilson asked, perplexed.

"Wilson, I didn't get to the rank of Chief by luck or eating donuts all day. There's a reason I'm the chief here. I am well aware of the possibilities and the ramifications. You would do well to know that I have contingencies in place. The way the knife showed up," the Chief explained, "I'd be a fool not to consider that angle! That is why I don't want you talking to anyone. This is all on a need-to-know basis. I don't know who the killer is now, but I know this is much more complicated than I ever thought."

"It was a cop," Wilson declared. "You know it, and I know it."

"That may be…."

"It was," Wilson insisted. "I talked to Cooper's parents, and…."

"You did what?" the Chief barked.

"I went to Cooper's parents and spoke with them."

"I don't recall clearing that, Detective Wilson."

"I know, but when I heard he had been sent home on paid leave, I had to talk to him," Wilson said, defending himself.

"Do you know why we have a chain of command, Wilson?" the Chief asked as his face turned the color of a ripe plum.

Wilson stood his ground, saying, "There was more to it, and I needed to know."

"We have a chain of command because sometimes hotshot detectives don't know as much as they think. We have a chain of command because sometimes lieutenants and chiefs have proved they can make better judgment calls than hotshot detectives who only see pieces of the puzzle while we see it all."

"Look, I'm sorry I didn't go through the bureaucratic process, but I was trying to track down a psychopath who hacked up an entire family. And in doing so, I found out that the person who left that knife at the scene had to have been another cop."

"Like Cooper?" the Chief asked in a mocking tone. "The kid you harassed has an alibi."

"No, like someone Cooper worked with or from the station he was buddies with. I don't know for sure, but I know that Cooper brought a cop with him into that deli, and that cop took the knife."

"Maybe it was someone trying to frame Cooper — someone who wanted him out of the picture," the Chief suggested.

"Who is Cooper a threat to?" Wilson asked, brushing off the Chief's suggestion. "You don't go after the low man on the totem pole when you get people out of your way."

"You've got the point there, Wilson. We probably won't know why they wanted to throw Cooper under the bus until we find out who it was. They probably didn't mean to get Cooper involved at all. Potentially, it was just luck on their part, throwing us off like that."

"If it was another cop, they meant to frame Cooper," Wilson said.

Wilson had not intended to tell the Chief about his theory yet, but with Michael Smith suddenly appearing out of nowhere, it seemed like vital information to share. Now he had to decide how much he would divulge. He wasn't sure if informing him about Laura doing some research on all the police on the scene would push the Chief over the edge.

Wilson didn't have to decide whether to tell the Chief about what he had Laura doing on the sly. He could see that the Chief was already about to put his head on the chopping block for talking to Cooper and his family. Before he could open his mouth again, there was a violent pounding on the Chief's door.

"Chief! Wilson! Please, open the door!"

It was Laura. She never acted that way. She was terrified of the Chief and usually did all she could to avoid him. Wilson was shocked to see her making a spectacle of herself on the other side of the Chief's door.

"Well, open the damn door before she breaks it down," the Chief ordered.

Wilson opened the door, pulled Laura into the office, and then slammed the door again so no one would see what was happening.

“This had better be important, dispatch,” the Chief growled.

“They found surveillance cameras at Declan Herring’s house!” she exclaimed, speaking so quickly that all the words slammed together.

“Why do you know this and I don’t?” the Chief asked.

“I overheard it on the radio. But that isn’t all,” Laura added.

Her eyes were two frenzied globes about to fly right off her face.

“There was only one officer who had worked the scene and didn’t have an alibi on the night the killings took place.”

“What the hell have you been up to, Laura?” the Chief roared. “And why don’t I know what is going on in my department?”

“It was Detective Stewart!” Laura exclaimed, disregarding the Chief’s anger.

Wilson’s heart flopped in his chest when he heard her name. He felt his stomach lurch, and his pupils swelled. Laura must have made a mistake.

“She was also the first to respond to the surveillance footage found just now.”

"It isn't Stewart," Wilson said as shock rattled through his body. "Stewart is a good detective; she's a good person."

"I'm sorry, Charlie, but she is the only one without an alibi so far," Laura repeated.

"So, she wasn't working that night. It doesn't make her a killer," Wilson snapped defensively. "And she's here, anyway, not out chasing down evidence to destroy it. I just saw her when I came in."

"I know she was here, but she left as soon as she heard about the surveillance film. She was standing by my office when it came in. I watched her dart off as soon as she heard it."

"When did you find out about the surveillance?" the Chief asked.

"Just now, ten minutes ago. That's why I made such a scene. If it was her, then…."

"Go, Wilson," the Chief ordered, cutting Laura off. "Go before Stewart gets there."

"You don't think it was her, do you?" Wilson asked, shaking his head. "I've known Stewart for a long time, and I can tell you she doesn't fit the bill."

"I don't know what to think, but I know that we have a suspect who may have been a victim sitting in a hospital downtown with a lot of evidence pointing at one of our own."

Wilson muttered, “It wasn’t her.”

“Now, I want you two to listen to me very carefully,” the Chief said before anyone left his office. “This does not go anywhere. I do not want any officer to know what is going on. If it is one of ours, a detective will be the best at escaping, so we will not tell anyone that we believe there is a suspect among us. Got it?”

“Yes, sir,” the two answered and turned to leave.

“I’m sorry, Charlie,” Laura whispered as they walked away.

Wilson didn’t answer her. He just kept walking until he was out of the office. Wilson headed for Herring’s house as the Chief called the officers who reported the surveillance footage not to release the evidence to anyone but Detective Wilson. He also pulled two more detectives who had not worked on the Arickson case to go with him to stand guard over Michael Smith. If it was indeed Detective Stewart — or any officer — it was only a matter of time before the guilty party showed up to silence the only possible living witness.

Smith had been too traumatized to speak to anyone yet, but the Chief felt what he might be told. The information that Smith would give the Chief would most likely put someone in prison for the rest of their life unless the surveillance video proved something different, of course.

10

The Evolution of a Monster

Stewart was already there when Wilson got to Herring's house. From yards away, he could see that she was irate. He felt a knot form in the pit of his stomach. He knew she wasn't the killer, but he also knew he had orders to follow, so he couldn't comfort her or tell her what was happening. Facing her was the last thing he wanted to do.

"Charles, thank God!" Stewart exclaimed as Wilson approached her.

On either side of her were two men —an officer and someone from forensics—who looked scared. Detective Stewart was small but terrifying when worked up. She was also stronger than most men in the force.

"These morons seem to think I'm not authorized to handle evidence in a case I'm working on. They claim that only *you* can retrieve it."

"Chief's orders," Wilson replied, sheepishly avoiding Cassidy's hot glare.

"What?" she snapped. "Is this some kind of sexist BS? I'm as much a part of this case as you are, Wilson, and you know that."

"Look, I don't know why the Chief does what he does," Wilson replied. "I just know I need to get the evidence back to the precinct."

"I'd like to know why!" Stewart insisted.

As she spoke, something came over her. She wasn't ferocious anymore. Something had changed in her demeanor that Wilson just couldn't put his finger on.

"You'll have to take it up with the Chief, Cass," Wilson answered apologetically. "Please don't shoot the messenger here. I can see you've already given these guys hell. You'll just have to go ask…."

"Why don't you cut the crap and tell me what is happening?" Stewart spat back.

"I'm sorry," Wilson replied, then turned to leave.

He wanted to be as far away from Cassidy Stewart and her fury as possible. Being in her presence was more than just uncomfortable; it was eating at his conscience. He couldn't stand lying to her. But most of all, he hated knowing what the Chief thought about her and not being able to tell her.

"I thought we were more than this," she said to Wilson as he got into his car. "I thought I meant more to you."

He didn't reply. He slammed his door shut, took a deep breath, and put the surveillance footage on the seat beside him.

"Please, Charles!" Stewart cried out.

Charles shuddered when he recognized the sound of desperation in her voice. The look that he had seen flash across her face earlier, he suddenly realized, was of fear.

She was afraid of something, but what? He couldn't wrap his head around what it all meant.

Wilson's phone rang as he sat silently in his car. A jumble of messy thoughts swirled around his head, jerking him from his restless contemplation. It was the Chief.

"Do you know where Stewart is?" the Chief asked before Wilson could even say hello.

"I'm staring at her," Wilson replied.

"Arrest her."

"What?"

"Now, Wilson. Make an arrest. I want her here in cuffs now."

"For what purpose?" Wilson said. "We have no evidence that even suggests that she has done something. You can't just arrest her because she is trying to work on a case. She…."

"Smith is awake and talking. He has identified Stewart as the person who abducted him."

"How could she have…."

"Now, Wilson!" the Chief said, his voice deep and commanding. "Before she gets the notion to make a run for it."

Wilson slammed his phone closed and threw it across his car. He looked over at Cassidy, who was heading for her car now.

"Stewart, wait," he called out.

"What?" she replied, standing with her hand on the handle of her car door.

"I need you to step away from your car," Wilson said as he put his hand near his pistol on his side.

"What is this, Charles?" she asked.

"Please, Cassidy, just step away from the car."

Stewart's eyes burned into Wilson's so intensely that he could feel them burning right through the back of his skull. He was about to tell her he was sorry and knew it was all a misunderstanding. Still, before opening his mouth again, Stewart jumped into her car and threw it into reverse. Her tires screamed as they burned charcoal-colored scars into the concrete driveway.

"Stop!" Wilson called out as Stewart flew past him, nearly running him over.

Wilson yanked his pistol from its holster and fired four shots. He blew out the two rear tires of Stewart's squad car, but she just kept going.

"Just call the Chief; tell him what is happening. She's a suspect," he shouted to the other officers at the scene, who were bewildered by what was transpiring.

One of them started for his car, but Wilson called out, "No! I got it," as he got into his car and took off for Stewart.

Wilson ripped through the quiet neighborhood after Stewart. She did not cover the kind of ground she needed to get away from him with two blown-out tires. Wilson got on the radio to try to convince her to stop.

"You aren't making this any better," he said.

She didn't answer. Wilson pressed the gas pedal harder. He was coming up fast on Stewart as they turned onto the main road. The metal axles of Stewart's car spit white-hot showers of sparks behind her as she tried to accelerate. It was an epic sight. She was riding out like a meteor, trailed by a dazzling glow. Just like a meteor, though, she would eventually burn up.

"Just stop, Cassidy," Wilson pleaded over the radio. "You are forcing me to do something I don't want to."

Still, she didn't respond. Wilson pounded his foot on the gas, slamming his car into Stewart's. The impact hurled Wilson so hard that the vinyl seat belt felt like it had cut through his skin. Stewart's car was catapulted to the shoulder of the road and then down a shallow ditch. Wilson barely kept control of his vehicle. He edged it to the shoulder and was out and running before Stewart's car had even come to a complete stop. He drew his gun and made his way to the vehicle, smashed like a soda can.

"How could you do it?" he called out as he approached the vehicle.

He could see that Stewart was slumped over in the seat when he got to the back of the car.

"Answer me!" he demanded.

He didn't want to believe she had done it, but he knew that only a guilty person would act the way she was acting. He couldn't lie to himself anymore. *Cassidy Stewart was the murderer.*

Wilson stood at the back of the car's driver's side and called again. "Get out of the car, Cassidy! Now! And I want to see your hands." Wilson took two cautious steps toward the car. "Are you conscious?" he asked.

Stewart's body didn't move. Wilson took another step toward the driver's side door, and just as he did, he saw Stewart lunge for the passenger door, swing the door open, and take off running.

"Damn it, Cassidy, I will shoot you if you don't stop!" Wilson yelled. He took off after his one-time colleague and longtime love interest.

Just then, Stewart stopped. She was standing beside Wilson's car by that time and froze.

"Hands up!" Wilson ordered, and Stewart slowly raised her hands.

Wilson jogged toward her so he could put her into cuffs. He watched as Stewart made a quick movement and dove into his car through the open driver's side door before making it to her.

Wilson holstered his gun in one quick motion and darted for the car. Stewart tried to close it on him just as he reached the door. He knew he had to stop Stewart from taking off and leaving him on foot.

"Stop this, Cassidy!" Wilson shouted as he threw himself into the car and wrapped his arms around her tiny waist, so she couldn't escape him again.

Stewart squirmed like a small lizard in the hand of a five-year-old, scrambling for the evidence bag sitting in the seat. With his hands wrapped around her, Wilson hurled himself backward to get her out of the car and onto the ground. The two went sailing back out of the car and landed hard on the asphalt. As they hit the ground, she drove both elbows hard into his gut, leaving Wilson breathless on the ground.

"Sttttttt…" Wilson tried calling out but couldn't get enough breath to do it.

"Just stay down, Wilson!" Stewart grunted as she jumped back into the car and reached for the bag with the evidence from the surveillance CD.

She fumbled with the pack, trying to get the CD out. Her fingers trembled as she tried to rip the bag open. It was too thick. She bit down on the plastic and tried to tear it with her teeth.

"Damn it!" she hissed as she fumbled with the evidence bag. "Come on!"

Wilson recovered from the blow to the abdomen and pounced on Stewart again. This time, he got her out of the car.

"You're making this worse, Stewart," he said between clenched teeth as he wrestled his ex-colleague out of the car.

Stewart was now pinned to the ground by Wilson. With the palms of his hands pressing on her back, he was straddling her. He softly pushed his legs against her back and grasped his cuffs to immobilize her. Stewart rolled over, now on her back, bringing Wilson crashing down on top of her. Now face to face.

Wilson's eye socket was crushed when she rammed her forehead against his right cheekbone. As his vision blurred on the right side and blood gushed from his face, he strained to hold her. Wilson took a knee to the groin from Stewart, who then rammed her balled fist into his throat. Wilson's windpipe collapsed, causing him to lose his breath. He was utterly unable to function. He knew Stewart was tough, but bringing her down was like battling a rabid leopard.

With Wilson unable to move, Stewart scrambled to her feet. She stood over Wilson, struggling on the ground to draw the tiniest of breaths. She pulled her 9mm pistol out and pointed it at Wilson.

"I didn't want to do this," she said. "Not to you, Charles. This was the last thing I wanted."

Wilson looked up at her as he gasped for air. Stewart cocked the gun and flipped the safety off. Her hand shook, and her eyes went glassy. She bit hard into her bottom lip and closed her eyes for a split second.

"Sorry, Charles," she said, but she dropped to the ground before letting loose hollow points to wreak havoc on Wilson's body.

Wilson saw Richard appear from behind her as she fell to the ground.

"You alright?" he asked as he jogged over.

Wilson sat up and rubbed his throat, shaking his head up and down. He finally caught his breath and thanked Detective Richard, who had sent fifty thousand volts of electricity from his Taser through Stewart before she could empty her magazine into Charles.

Wilson rubbed his throat, choking out the words, "Put her in cuffs."

"Gladly," Richard replied as he turned the stunned woman over and snapped handcuffs onto her birdlike wrists. "I can't even believe this is happening."

"Where's the CD?" Wilson asked as he pulled himself to his feet.

"The what?"

"The CD. It's the surveillance from Herring's place. It's in an evidence bag," Wilson answered, scanning the ground for the coveted evidence Stewart had been trying to tear into. "She was trying to destroy it just before she caved my windpipe in."

"Once I get her in the car, I'll help you look," Richard said, dragging Stewart off as she slowly recovered from the Taser jolt.

The two found the surveillance footage in the mangled evidence bag under Wilson's seat when he returned. Wilson studied the CD, ensuring that Stewart hadn't cracked or scratched it too severely.

"Looks good, considering what just happened," Richard said over Wilson's shoulder.

"I'll be interested to see what's on it," Wilson said.

"I'd say there is something pretty serious on it, by the fight she put up to get it."

As the two stood in silence, trying to digest everything that had just happened, a noise came from Richard's squad car and cut into their reflection. The sound rattled them both to their cores. The two spun around in unison and saw that the back window of Richard's car was smeared with crimson. It was blood—Stewart's blood.

"What in the hell?" Richard yelled out as he dashed to his car.

Wilson followed close behind him.

"What is it?" Wilson asked apprehensively as Richard peered into the backseat. "Is she…."

"Just knocked out cold, I think," Richard replied. "Looks like she bashed her head into the window, trying to get out."

"Or maybe trying to kill herself," Wilson mumbled.

"I'm going to open the door to check on her, so be prepared for anything."

"That's an understatement today," Wilson said as he braced himself, gun drawn and ready.

"She's alive; it's a pretty good laceration," Richard said over his shoulder.

He had two fingers on Stewart's neck, checking for a pulse. When he found she had a strong heartbeat, he leaned in further to examine the wound on her head. Wilson let himself relax as Richard checked the wound on Stewart's skull, but he kept his 9mm pistol in hand and his eyes on Richard.

"Do you think she needs to go to the hospital?" Wilson asked.

"It doesn't look that bad — just superficial. A head wound always looks worse because of all the blood," Richard replied, and just after the last syllable left his mouth, his legs started thrashing.

"Shit!" a muffled cry came from within the car.

Wilson lunged in to pull Richard out. He kept his gun in his right hand and grabbed a handful of Richard's shirt with his left. Richard heaved himself into Wilson, slamming the car door as he tumbled back onto Wilson.

"She bit me!" he cried as he groped at his right ear. "That crazy psychopath just took a chunk out of my ear!"

Wilson's gaze was drawn away from Richard's swollen earlobe and toward Stewart. Richard's blood glistened on her lips like candy-apple-colored lipstick while she sat with her blood matted into her blond hair. Wilson couldn't believe his eyes. Wilson had been smitten with this woman since he first met her. She was attractive, powerful, and successful. He thought she was exactly the kind of woman he would choose if he ever wanted to get settled down. For the first time in his life, the perfect image he had of her was shattered. In a million tiny shards, the remains of who she was, were strewn about him.

Only the crazy killer in front of him remained — a desperate and possessed woman. She'd transformed from a mystical creature into a gruesome horror movie monster. Wilson had seen a lot of horrible situations in his time; he had seen some of humanity's worst characters, but seeing Stewart was the worst yet because he knew what she had been like before. He knew the image of her, crazy and bleeding, would linger in his mind for a long time, possibly forever.

"Who are you?" Wilson asked as he leaned down and gazed inward at this broken human being.

Stewart didn't say a word. She sat as still as a gargoyle, posted eternally on the mossy steps of a centuries-old fortress. She did not blink. Wilson could tell that she had not even taken a breath. She only sat there, as if catatonic, looking at him. Her stare chilled Wilson to the depths of his being. Her eyes seemed almost vacant, but there was something ominous in them. Something in them told Wilson that whatever humanity was left in her had leaped out or vanished into her darkness.

"What made you become this?" he asked after she had sat motionless for what seemed like years.

"Pain," she replied.

Wilson could not hear her clearly through the window, but he could see what she said in the movement of her lips.

"What pain?" Wilson asked.

Stewart jerked her head forward and fell back into her unblinking stare.

"You need to go get stitched up?" Wilson asked Richard as he walked over to him.

"I think I'll be fine," he replied. "Take a look and see what you think," he said, taking his hand off his bleeding ear.

Wilson flinched and exclaimed, "Jeez!"

"Is it that bad?"

"It probably doesn't need stitches, but that is a nasty wound you got there," Wilson told him. "I can't believe she did that."

"She's a damn wild animal." Richard shook his head.

"I think she might be something more sinister than that," Wilson replied, looking back toward the squad car.

"Whatever she is, she shouldn't be allowed to walk the streets anymore," Richard said with a chuckle.

Wilson replied, "At least not in this lifetime."

"Charles, is everything OK? Over." It was Laura, coming over the radio.

Wilson reached down for his phone and realized he didn't know where it had gone. The Chief had probably been calling to check on the situation with Stewart. He jogged toward his car to answer Laura.

"I'm here," he said. "Over."

"Is everything all right? We heard that Stewart fled, and then there was nothing. Over."

"I'm fine," Wilson answered. "Richard showed up. He's missing a piece of his ear, but we're both fine, and Stewart is cuffed and in a squad car. We're about to head that way. Over."

"What happened to Richard's ear?" Laura asked.

"Stewart. Over."

"What do you mean, *Stewart*? Over."

"I'll explain after we have her booked and get a chance to look at whatever is on this video," he told her. "Over."

"Mind if I take her in?" Wilson asked as he and Richard prepared to leave.

"Be my guest, man," he replied. "I'd rather not ride with that psychotic cannibal anyway."

"I'll see you back at the station," Wilson said and got into Richard's car to take his longtime dream woman to be fingerprinted, strip-searched, and put in a concrete cage.

"Why did you do it?" Wilson asked as they drove.

"Do what?" Stewart asked.

"Why did you kill the Aricksons?"

"I didn't," she answered.

"So, what is all this about, then?"

"You all are trying to pin something on me. I was trying to escape," she replied calmly. "It's called survival."

"You thought this was the best way to handle it?"

"What would you have me do, Charles?"

"About a thousand other things other than this," he said. "An innocent person doesn't run. You know that."

"Who's innocent these days?" she asked, staring forward past the car's hood into eternity.

"What's in the video you don't want us to see?"

"I don't know what you're talking about," she replied coldly.

"You were trying to get to that CD. What is on it that you don't want us to see?" Wilson asked again.

"I still don't know what you're talking about, Charles."

"We'll all know soon enough," Wilson said. "Go ahead and keep it to yourself now, but we'll all know soon."

"We'll see," she whispered.

11

The Truth Shall Set Them Free

Wilson arrived at the station to a congregation of all the on-duty officers in the precinct. The high-profile case brought the media into the loop, and it became a shit show. The entire country's attention was on the case, and in a situation like that, it was damning for them to have one of their own as the perp. The department wasn't new to facing crooked cops and wayward outlaws now and again, but this was a first.

Wilson was unsure whether he wanted to play such a pivotal role in the matter. In this case, along with the dynamics between himself and Cassidy and the whole deception angle, Wilson wouldn't be surprised if it was turned into a Hollywood movie. This was the second case after the shooting of Biggie and 2Pac that garnered this much attention. The Arickson case was as high-profile as a case could get when it came to the jurisdiction of the police department.

Wilson couldn't help but wonder what it would be like for Cassidy once word got out. If the press got hold of this, her face would officially become the most recognized face in the state, if not the country.

One of their associates was now held as the primary suspect, making the situation a shambles for the department.

Wilson internally said a quick prayer of blessing for the demise of the Chief's job.

"You want to tell me what is on the footage before we go in?" Wilson asked, turning to Stewart one last time before they got out of the car.

"How could I possibly know?" Stewart replied.

"Suit yourself, Stewart," he said.

As people and reporters gathered, the Chief sent out a large group of uniformed officers to keep people away while Wilson walked Stewart to the station. Wilson looked at the crowd gathered and couldn't help but wonder if these useless fuckers didn't have anything better to do on a Tuesday afternoon.

"Don't these fuckers have anything better to do?" Stewart said just as Wilson was about to open the door.

He looked down and chuckled. He couldn't help but admit that they had undeniable chemistry. He opened the door, holding Stewart by the arm. He guided her through the swarm of people and the press as the officers did their best to hold them off.

"Someone's going to throw garbage at us!" Stewart whispered, leaning into Wilson.

Barely a second later, Wilson pulled her out of the way as he saw an incoming projectile.

"I've got you," Wilson instinctively said.

"Do you?" Stewart replied, her lips curling in the most casual style.

Wilson was taken aback by the comment. He looked ahead and pulled her in through the gates of the station.

"I wonder what they're doing here," Stewart said, shaking off Wilson's arm as she bent down to brush some dirt off her knee.

Wilson quickly caught hold of her.

"For fuck's sake, Cassidy!" he whispered fiercely, knowing everybody had just seen the action.

"Oh, it's Cassidy now?"

Wilson pulled her arm, causing her to stumble, and quickly led her to the elevator leading up to the precinct's second floor. The doors closed, and the two of them were finally alone for a moment.

"Do you think I did it?" Stewart asked, her tone noticeably different.

Wilson didn't answer.

"I see."

Wilson didn't answer.

The elevator reached the second floor, and the doors opened. Thankfully, this area was a bit emptier—just the detectives, all of whom had the subtlety of a drunk redneck. They all stood at their desks, looking at them.

The detectives on the desks further from the lift took the liberty of forming a line along the elevator.

"Hi guys, this is Cassidy Stewart. I'm sure you've all met her. I can assure you that she is still the same Cassidy Stewart and has not changed in the past two days you didn't see her, alright?" Wilson said it aloud, holding Cassidy by the arm alongside him.

The detectives took the hint and dispersed, although they didn't hold back the inevitable, "What the fuck? Are they in love?"

Wilson looked straight ahead and pulled Cassidy along to the interrogation room. Thankfully, nobody was waiting for them in the interrogation room to get a glimpse.

Wilson walked Cassidy over to the perp side of the table and sat her down.

Cassidy walked to the opposite end and sat on the seat, pulling herself in and flicking her hair out of her face.

"Don't make this harder than it has to be. You still have people on your side," Wilson said, looking at Cassidy, who resolutely refused to meet his eyes.

This time, she didn't answer.

Wilson heard a knock, and the door opened. The Chief's secretary stepped in.

"Chief needs you," she said, smiling awkwardly.

She quickly exited the room and slammed the door shut.

Wilson took one last look at Stewart and saw her looking at her lap. He left the room and headed straight for the Chief's office. He could feel the eyes of his coworkers bore a hole in the back of his skull as he entered.

"Chief," Wilson said, opening the door.

"Jesus Christ, this is a cluster fuck," the Chief said, looking out of his window.

Wilson nodded knowingly, "My thoughts exactly."

"I'm going to get her booked," the Chief said.

Wilson frowned at that. It was uncharacteristic of the Chief to be so biased.

"You know the kind of pressure I'm under because Stewart decided to become a killer!" he said, looking angrily at Wilson as if he were also responsible.

Wilson didn't say anything.

"My orders, Chief?" he said, feeling glad that he wasn't the one making calls right now.

"The Coopers are in holding room three. You take care of them."

"The Coopers?" Wilson asked, confused.

"Sergeant Waters will catch you up," the Chief answered.

"Chrissy!" The Chief said unnaturally loudly. "Get Waters in here!"

Wilson gave an unnaturally formal salute to the Chief and then left the room to meet Sergeant Waters. Sergeant Waters was a stout man with swollen forearms who wore too much hair gel. He had been pulled into the case as it unraveled and became more complicated since they needed the manpower. He was a flamboyant guy, but he was trustworthy.

"What's the deal with the Coopers?" Wilson asked, not wasting a second as they walked toward holding room three.

"We have them here to identify Stewart," he told Wilson.

"*Identify* Stewart?"

"Yeah, we have Smith's testimony, but everything else appears circumstantial," Waters explained.

"Biting an officer's ear off and fleeing a scene is hardly circumstantial," Wilson scoffed.

"You and I know that lawyers can make about anything circumstantial. You're almost guaranteed a not-guilty verdict unless you have a confession or a video of a murderer killing someone. And even with hard evidence, a good enough lawyer can get past it once reality kicks in. It's innocent until proven guilty — beyond the shadow of a doubt."

"Good point, I suppose," Wilson responded.

"So, we need to gather as much as we can to keep her in. We know a knife came from the Coopers' deli at the scene. If the Coopers can identify her, we'll have a better shot. That gives Smith's account more weight, too. With his DNA at the scene, it would be easy to discount him, unless…."

"Unless we have enough evidence from other places tying Stewart to the murders."

Wilson couldn't understand what was going on. According to history, the department has gone out of its way to implicate one of its own. They cited insanity if all else failed. It felt like they were tasked with making Cassidy guilty this time around.

"Bingo," Waters said.

"Let me get this CD to evidence, and then I'll go," Wilson said as the two made it through the homicide department.

Wilson dropped the surveillance footage off and told the lab technician to let him know when it was ready to watch. He also requested a few pictures of Stewart for him to show to the Coopers. Once he had the photos of Stewart, he headed for holding room three to talk to the Coopers.

"Hello again, Mr. and Mrs. Cooper," Wilson said as he entered the room, photos in hand. "I don't know if you remember me. My name is Detective Wilson. I interviewed you just a week ago or so."

"We remember you, detective," Mr. Cooper replied. "You work with Jason. You showed us the pictures of those men."

"That's right, and I have a couple more questions for you," Wilson said, sitting across from them. "I have some more photos to show you. I want to see if you recognize the person in these."

Wilson laid out the pictures on the tables for the couple. Wilson could see the recognition in their eyes before they even uttered a word, and his heart sank instantly. However, he remembered that he had been worried about their memories after their last conversations.

"That's Jason's friend; they went to school together," Mrs. Cooper said with certainty. "I always thought they'd make such a nice couple."

"How long has it been since you've seen her in the deli?" Wilson asked, gritting his teeth as he realized the implications of their testimony.

"Oh, it's difficult to say," Mrs. Cooper responded. "Maybe two weeks. But, last time, she came in alone. She said she just loved our sandwiches." The old woman beamed.

"Did she come in often?" Wilson asked.

"Not often, per se. Just a couple of times with Jason and then that time by herself. She bought a whole pound of sliced turkey and a deli knife from us the last day she was here. She said she'd like to have it as a souvenir. I was a bit surprised she didn't come back since she likes our sandwiches so much."

"Probably just busy," Wilson said, forcing a smile.

His head pounded as he looked at them.

Something about Mrs. Cooper made Wilson's heart hurt a little. He had gotten good at detaching himself from cases and the people involved, but as he sat with that older woman and saw the naïveté she possessed and her trust, he felt pained and a bit angry.

The sensation was unsettling for the seasoned detective. It was something foreign to him, and he wanted it to leave. The feeling haunted him because he saw traces of himself in the witness for the first time since he had become a detective. He had fallen into a trap that he always thought he'd be able to avoid, hitting him like a truck. He could never imagine being deceived by someone he trusted so much. He was a gullible bystander to all of Stewart's lies. His emotional ties to her had made him like all the pathetic family members and close friends he had interviewed over the years while chasing after the refuse of society.

As Mrs. Cooper continued about the deli and Cassidy, Wilson's eyes were fixed on the photograph. The

Cassidy Stewart he had grown to know and love stared back at him through the photos, but the current Cassidy was completely different. He couldn't reconcile the dual pictures of her in his mind.

The Cassidy he knew was a good detective and a good woman. The Cassidy he knew now was not the same one capable of biting a chunk out of a colleague's ear with her bare teeth. The contrast between Cassidy, who solved countless cases with him and flirted with him in the elevator every morning, proved to be a hard one to come to terms with. It struck Wilson how much a person could change overnight.

Or, Wilson thought, *she was simply good at disguising who she was.* Wilson was taken by the fact that Cassidy was always there, lurking in the cobwebbed corners of his psyche, popping up in dreams and surfacing in white-hot flashes of rage quickly tamped out. Wilson had seen her angry several times. He always saw it as a sign of her passion, but maybe it was a sign of this monster waiting to break through. He wondered if anything Cassidy ever told him was true.

"Why do you folks want to know when she came in?" Mr. Cooper asked.

"Excuse me?" Wilson spoke distractedly, trying to silence all his thoughts so he could finish the interview.

"Well," Wilson began but paused.

He didn't know if he could bring himself to shatter their image of the girl they'd known from the time she was a teenager. His world had been turned upside down because of her.

But did theirs have to be as well? Would it be a favor to them to let them live in ignorance? Or is it not my call to make? But then again... ignorance is bliss.

Wilson struggled with the moral dilemma for a while but realized that he was only going through it because he had feelings for this girl. He allowed his emotions to cloud his judgment because he would never have had the same debate with himself in any other case.

"Yes?" Mr. Cooper replied, waiting for Wilson to finish his thought.

"She's a suspect in a murder case," he said, still gritting his teeth. *I have morals, but I also have a heart.* He told himself.

Regardless, they were adults and didn't need him to protect them. The world was tough, and Wilson wasn't there to soften its edges. He was there to do his job.

"We think she was involved in the case I talked to you about earlier — the Arickson murders."

"A *suspect* for the Aricksons' murders?" Mrs. Cooper gasped in disbelief. "She's a sweet girl. You must be mistaken."

“I hope so,” Wilson forced a half-smile and told the Coopers they were free to go.

Wilson walked out without another word and turned back to the Chief, lost in thought.

“Wilson, you need to get in here now,” Richard said as Wilson walked past the lab.

“HEY! Wilson!” the lab tech yelled to get his attention.

Wilson did a double-take and turned around.

“Is that from the surveillance footage?” he asked, connecting the dots.

Richard nodded and said, “You should mentally prepare yourself for this, man. I wish someone had warned me.”

Wilson pushed past Richard to get to the film room. When he got there, he could see that Richard was not speaking nonsense. The expressions on the faces of all the detectives in the room told him that whatever he was going to see would probably rocket to the top of his trauma list. It takes a bit to shock a roomful of detectives, and well… this was a bit. Whatever was on the footage was anything but run-of-the-mill, even for a homicide department. Wilson felt all the contents of his stomach bubble up to the back of his throat. He wasn’t sure he wanted to see something that stunned a group used to pulling bloated bodies out of rivers and examining gunshot victims.

"I want to watch it alone," Wilson announced before one of the lab guys could play the footage.

"You sure?" asked the lab technician.

"Yes," Wilson said, confirming. "Whatever it is, I'd rather see it alone."

"Alright, sir. But get ready, OK? It'll mess you up good."

Wilson gave the nod. Once everyone left, he closed the film room door with the remote control. For some reason, the remote felt heavier than an anvil. He studied the small silver apparatus. Once he pushed the play button, there was no going back. Wilson thought it was strange how significant something so ordinary had suddenly become. That remote would lift the final veil from his eyes. It would throw him into a harsh reality he had never dealt with. He knew whatever was on the footage would change him.

Wilson squeezed his eyes shut and pressed the button on the remote. The button felt electrically charged. He slammed it down on the desk beside him. He sat quietly and watched the footage. He recognized the image on the screen; it was the back side of Declan Herring's house. The detective sat silently, not moving a muscle. To the best of his ability, he did everything he could to prepare for what he was about to witness.

After a few minutes, Declan emerged onto the back porch. He sat down in an old rocking chair made of wood on his patio and lit a cigarette. The act made Wilson grab his electronic cigarette and wish for the real thing. He took deep drags off the device as he watched Declan sit in the glow of his porch light, taking drags off his cigarette for a minute or two. Everything appeared to be calm and peaceful until Declan rose abruptly from his chair.

Although there was no sound in the video, Wilson could see that Declan was talking to someone outside the frame. He looked angry as he spoke, but the anger quickly dissipated and turned into fear. Declan began backing toward the door. As he grabbed for the door handle, a figure attacked him; it was the person Declan was talking to. He had a smaller stature but was more powerful. The two struggled. The attacker's hand grasped something and, with a powerful swing, plunged it into Declan. It was a knife, of course. Declan's motions slowed for a moment, then got erratic.

Wilson squinted to get a better look at the assailant. He already knew who he was, but unless the footage picked up his face, he knew it would not be beneficial to them. He watched closely to see if she ever turned to the camera. As he watched, the scene got worse. It was apparent that the figure was a woman. The assailant turned Declan over, hovering over him with a foot on either side of his body. She pulled out handcuffs from her pocket and snapped the cuffs on the victim. Declan must have screamed because next, the attacker put a hand over his mouth. Thereafter, she leaned in and whispered something to him, then stood up, pulled her knife out of his body, and slit his throat swiftly. The pavement went dark with his blood.

Wilson winced as Declan's body went limp. He wanted to look away, but he had to see if the assailant turned around to expose who she was. He kept his eyes locked on the screen, hoping that the worst was over, but it wasn't. The woman began kicking the victim over and over. When she finally stopped, she stepped back. There it was, her face. It was Cassidy. Wilson looked right into her eyes. It was that vacant expression from the car. Chills gripped him, but still, he kept watching.

Wilson could see the victim was still barely breathing. The next second, the woman sat on the victim's chest and snapped his neck in one swift motion. The remainder of the footage showed Stewart dragging his body away, cleaning the porch, so no blood was left, and then disappearing into the house. Wilson knew exactly what she was doing; she was creating a scene for them to find. She went inside to make it appear as if Herring had left town in a hurry.

Once it was apparent that Stewart was done with her murderous exploit, Wilson turned the footage off and sat for a moment in silence. *Why?* He wondered. *Why would she do this?* Answering that question would be his next quest.

***

Wilson walked out of the room in a daze. He could feel the eyes of every detective in the precinct on him. It wasn't so much what he saw on the footage – he'd definitely seen the worst that humanity had to offer, and despite that, it was still one of the worst things he'd ever seen. It wasn't so much about the way that Cassidy went about performing the murders, but the fact was that it was her doing it.

In all of Wilson's wildest imaginations, he had never thought Cassidy was ever capable of doing something like that, but it turned out that not only was she the culprit, but she was also very smart about the way she went about doing it. Wilson couldn't think straight. He was about to enter the investigation room, where Cassidy was waiting when a flood of emotions hit him. Something within him stopped him just as he was about to turn the doorknob.

Wilson didn't want to go in there with a head full of steam because he knew that it would just make Cassidy understand that she was in charge of the situation, and that would just majorly set them back. But at the same time, he wanted to throw caution to the wind. He wanted Cassidy to be in front of him so that he could talk to her about everything.

Deciding to go with the latter, he burst through the door and decided to get into it instantly with Cassidy, who was still handcuffed to the desk. Wilson locked the door behind him and took a seat opposite Cassidy.

"You know what kind of time you're facing? I don't understand why you're not letting me help you out when I know I'm going to do right by you!"

Wilson spat at the girl sitting handcuffed to the desk. For a moment, he thought he saw the icy exterior break to reveal the still soft and moral person he once knew and worked with. But it had gone just as fast as it came. Regardless of the fact that it was gone, he knew it had still been there.

"The fact that you locked the door on your own tells me that you don't really have any right being here, do you?" Cassidy asked.

"Cut the shit, Stewart. I just watched you snap a man's neck. I want to know why!"

"You just watched *someone* snap a guy's neck," she said, correcting him.

He snarled, "I just watched *you*. I'm not playing those interrogation games to get you to talk. If you like, I can show you the footage. Your face is crystal clear. I'm sure if you knew there was a camera just above you, you might have used a mask. A rookie mistake, I guess. You were at least competent enough to plant prints and other evidence. All that planning and preparation, and you're still going down because of a sloppy error."

Wilson saw a change in her demeanor. He knew that look well from past criminals he had busted. She knew she was caught. It was almost like a death rattle. That look was the final sign, as it meant that she realized it was over.

"Tell me why," he insisted.

"I want to see my lawyer," Stewart responded.

Her eyes were filled with tears.

"Forget about your lawyer! You know your damn rights," Wilson shouted.

"Explain to me why you did it. And why Arickson?"

"I didn't do anything to Arickson," she claimed. "There's nothing that ties me to that. You're all on a witch hunt right now."

"On a witch hunt!" Wilson yelled. "We've been on a witch hunt, chasing after clues you planted, but we've finally caught our witch."

"I had nothing to do with Arickson," she insisted.

"Strange that you bought a knife from a sweet old couple right before the murder, and we recovered it at the scene. What made you buy the knife if you had nothing to do with it? It was a sloppy piece of work indeed."

"It is surprising for a detective as good as you, Stewart. I must admit that I am a little disappointed. You almost had it, though, Cass. You broke into Arickson's residence without the maid knowing. I should have picked up on the fact that you knew where the master bedroom was and which side of the bed Steven Arickson slept on. I suppose I was too blinded by the fact that I thought you were a decent human being. Cassidy, I just don't get it. I don't get what transformed you into this monster."

"He lied to me!" Stewart shouted, slamming her fists on the table.

The outburst startled Wilson.

"Who?"

"Steven, he lied. He caused all this, not me."

"What are you talking about?" Wilson probed.

"He was supposed to leave her. They weren't happy. I made him happy. But then he called it off, saying that I needed to get on with my life. He lied to me. He loved me, and I loved him. But he wasn't brave enough to leave," she bellowed.

"So, you killed his entire family? You're even worse than I thought."

"I warned him," she spat. "I told him what I would do if he didn't leave them. I said that he would be the reason they all died. All he had to do was keep his promise, and they'd be here. But he didn't. He lied. He was the one who committed the sin, but they all had to pay the price for it."

"So, that's what the message was about."

"He did it," she cried, "not me!"

"You killed six innocent people, nearly seven, because of a crush? You are not at all who I thought you were, Cassidy. I used to think you were stronger than anyone I knew, but really, you're pathetic."

"People like us don't find love easily," she said, her gaze fixed on Wilson. Her voice was suddenly steady, and she appeared strangely calm. "I found it and wasn't going to let it go."

When Stewart used the phrase "people like us," Wilson recoiled. She was implying that they were the same. He could never be like her; she was a monster. What she had done was heinous. He was not cut from the same cloth as someone who could murder innocent people, including children. The very thought of them being similar in any way turned his stomach.

"Don't ever assume that *we* are alike!" Wilson exploded.

"We are, and you know it, Charlie," Stewart remarked sarcastically, emphasizing his name. "We were so much alike that it was impossible for us to even find a way to fall in love."

"We're nothing alike. You are a killer, and I am a cop."

"I was a cop, too, Charles. And I tell you, it wasn't as hard as I thought to switch sides."

"That's because you have evil inside of you."

Stewart just rolled her eyes and scoffed. "There is no such thing as evil, Charles. There are people who stand on one side of a line; that's all. And with people like you and me who make chasing down killers our life—people who don't love, feel, or connect with other people because we're too busy investigating murders. It's not hard to step right over that line."

"Why did you kill Herring, too?" Wilson asked, changing the subject. "He had nothing to do with it."

"It's easier to pin a crime on a person if it seems like they fled town."

"So why didn't you kill Smith?"

"He got away," she explained. "I couldn't just kill him at his house like I did Herring. Between his wife and his security system, it was impossible. So, I took him out to the sticks, and he got away, but I'm sure he'll tell you all that."

"I believe I'm done here," Wilson stated. "And so are you."

"So, Charles, what's next? Now that you have caught the killer, what are your plans?"

Charles paused to consider the question. He thought about how deranged Cassidy had become. She had trained herself not to feel like a human; therefore, she stopped being one. He wasn't going to risk losing the rational part of himself any longer. The repercussions were far too severe. He was going to make changes so that no one could ever accuse him of being anything like the lunatic sitting before him.

"I'm going to ask a cute barista out on a date," he answered.

"Be careful," Stewart cautioned as Wilson got up to leave. "Love can be tricky."

"I'll take my chances," he replied. "I don't want to end up a deranged killer because I shut myself off from the rest of the world."

"Well, best of luck," Stewart said.

"And good luck in prison," Wilson said as he shut the door behind him.

12

Can You Make One

Almost immediately, the press descended. The story was too good to pass up. Wilson could imagine tomorrow's newspaper headlines reading, *A Gruesome Murder. A Sex Scandal! A gorgeous female police officer is at the center of it all.*

If the presidents of CNN, MSNBC, and Fox News had gotten together in a smokey room and constructed a sordid tale to draw in viewers, they wouldn't have been able to invent anything better. Sometimes, reality has the bad habit of becoming more entertaining than fiction.

Wilson, the lead detective and the suspect's partner, found himself at the center of it all. He was not a guy who cared much for the limelight. Wilson enjoyed his quiet life, his apartment, and his few work friends. He never had any interest in being famous, but it was thrust upon him.

The local news crews were the first to call. One evening, a hack named Phillips, who had spent his entire career looking for anything to smear the police department, showed up at Wilson's building. He tracked Wilson down and tried to play it as if they were fast friends, even bringing up a complex case that Wilson had worked on, which he covered. Of course, Wilson remembered reading that article, and he'd been shocked to find himself referred to as a "clueless cop" or "pretty boy," as he happily reminded Phillips. Wilson had had enough when the constant refusals didn't work and had Phillips escorted off the premises by two uniformed officers. Fortunately, nothing became violent, which was a win in his book.

Marquez, oddly enough, stayed out of the fray. He ran into her a couple of days after the arrest.

She gave him a look and said, "I told you she was trouble."

Wilson didn't have anything to say about that. He was pleasantly surprised by how balanced her stories on the matter ended up being, even if they went on far longer than he would have liked.

Next came the national guys. Wilson politely told him to stuff it. He even got the president of MSNBC to call his line one afternoon. Supposedly, that thing worked all the time, impressed the marks, and got them to agree to satellite feeds and appearances.

Finally, the agents arrived, and the guys were looking to capitalize on it all. They came bearing promises of fame and fortune, book deals, and unique appearance fees as an expert guest on various news programs. They swore he'd never have to work a real job again, which they didn't realize was the exact opposite of what Wilson desired.

Despite his best attempts at escaping the limelight, he became famous anyway, more so because he tried to avoid it. He didn't give people a chance to get tired of him.

Wilson realized how much the case had already impacted his life when the Chief ordered him to spend his time in the spotlight because it was either him or Stewart. And she was already eating up enough airtime as it was.

With her, the media tried everything. They referred to her as a seductress or a siren. Nancy Grace also referred to her in other, less flattering ways.

She did, however, have websites dedicated to her. Men all over the country were picking apart her looks, making crude jokes about whether she was worth killing for. They referenced the Fireburner. Late-night talk show hosts couldn't go a night without working her into their monologues. Groups sprang up, calling for her release.

Wilson wanted to personally visit each of those groups, bringing photos of the crime scene and a copy of the video of what she did to Herring. He wanted the rest of the world to know that she wasn't some misunderstood feminist or sexual fantasy. She was a cold-blooded murderer.

Cooper returned sometime during the whole mess. The entire squad went out of their way to make him feel like a part of the team. He seemed grateful to be back, yet hollow-eyed and wary. The odd, inappropriate jokes had vanished. Wilson could tell he still had something in his heart for Stewart. It was difficult to ignore his little glances at the now-empty desk.

"You have to drop it, kid," Wilson finally said one day.

"Drop what?"

Wilson grimaced and nodded toward Stewart's old spot.

"Whatever your motivation for joining the force, you have the makings of an excellent cop. But you must let her go. You know that, right?"

Cooper nodded but remained silent for a moment. Sometimes, a man just needs some silence to ponder. Wilson left him alone.

"I'm not sure how."

"How what?" Wilson inquired.

"How can I be a good cop, Detective? After all that time, I didn't see any of it. I had absolutely no idea."

"None of us did," Wilson assured him.

Cooper agreed, "Yeah."

But it was apparent he disagreed. Not really. In his heart, no.

"Look, Cooper, you must understand that you can't know what's happening inside people. There is only so much that people show you. You'll see it again and again if you keep doing this line of work. You'll spend your entire career attempting to see through the masks. And you'll get better; you must if you want to succeed. But no matter how long you stay—and some of these guys have been around since the dinosaurs walked the earth — there will always be things you don't get to witness. Sometimes not until it's too late."

He realized the speech was as much for himself as it was for Cooper because, deep down, he had been feeling the same way. It didn't do much for him, but he was older. He'd seen a lot more. The kid was still green enough that it would make him feel better. Only time will tell.

The squad room was quiet for a long time after the case. Even when the verdict came down — life in prison, no chance of parole — there wasn't any celebrating. Wilson was in the courthouse when it happened. That much he felt he owed the Arickson family. Stewart sat with her head down the entire time. Her legs sagged a bit when the judge read the verdict, but she didn't make a sound. Her eyes were glassy and lifeless. When she spotted Wilson, she gave him a curt nod. It was as if it were the old days, and they were just passing each other in the booking area. He didn't know what to make of that, but it left him cold.

***

The day he found himself in the coffee shop, things were starting to calm down. He was admiring the barista with the piercing. The local newspaper was running a story about a political scandal. It involved a state senator with an apartment and a lady on the side. It was sufficiently juicy to divert everyone's attention.

Wilson was relieved to be back to just working cases. There was a simplicity to it. You got the call, investigated the scene, collected evidence, and started your search. It was almost always something petty and small, and it never amounted to what the Arickson case did. It felt familiar and put him at ease.

But that was also part of the problem. Everything was back to normal — as if nothing had changed. Yet, in truth, everything had changed. Everything was different.

He waited patiently for his turn in line, considering his last thought. It wasn't entirely accurate; not everything had changed. The world was the same. The job remained the same. Everything remained the same except for him.

"Morning, Detective," the barista chirped, flashing a wide smile. "The usual?"

He nodded, but his thoughts were elsewhere. She turned around and started making his drink. Was it his imagination, or did she put a little extra shake in her movements for him?

She came back after a few moments. Wilson's drink was ready to go. He felt her soft, gentle fingers brush against him as he received the coffee.

It occurred to him that things had changed and that he had changed. Then he realized that not all change has to be bad.

"Is there anything else I can get for you?"

He noticed the little extra twist she added to those lines for the first time. He looked deeply into her eyes and smiled.

"Yeah." *What the hell?* He thought. "How about your phone number?"

For a moment, she appeared befuddled, and he wondered whether he'd misread everything. But then her smile widened, too.

"My God," she exclaimed, "it's about time."

Made in the USA
Las Vegas, NV
27 February 2023